Sled Dog School

Sled Dog School

By Terry Lynn Johnson

HOUGHTON MIFFLIN HARCOURT
BOSTON   NEW YORK

hmhco.com

The text was set in Guardi.

The Library of Congress has cataloged the hardcover edition as follows:
Library of Congress Cataloging-in-Publication Data
Names: Johnson, Terry Lynn, author.
Title: Sled Dog School / by Terry Lynn Johnson.
Description: Boston ; New York : Houghton Mifflin Harcourt, [2017]
Summary: When eleven-year-old Matt must set up a business to save his failing
math grade, he overcomes his self-doubt and also gains two friends along the way.
Identifiers: LCCN 2016045212
Subjects: | CYAC: Dogsledding—Fiction. | Sled dogs—Fiction. |
Dogs—Training—Fiction. | Friendship—Fiction. | Business
enterprises—Fiction. | Alaska—Fiction.
Classification: LCC PZ7.J63835 Sle 2017 | DDC [Fic]—dc23
LC record available at https://lccn.loc.gov/2016045212

ISBN: 978-0-544-87331-5 hardcover
ISBN: 978-0-358-00456-1 paperback

Printed in the United States of America
DOC 10 9 8 7 6 5
4500781250

For everyone who has loved a dog

Sled Dog School

One

Matt didn't have much time.

"Haw," he called to his leaders, Foo and Grover, as they approached the fork in the trail. At the sound of his voice, the dogs' ears swiveled back. It made Matt proud that they listened to him the same way they listened to his dad, even though Matt was eleven.

The team didn't break stride as they charged down the left trail. Matt loved watching them charge. When the dogs were happy, he was happy. Most times.

The wind grabbed the scarf Matt's dad had made for him and whipped him in the face. He wouldn't wear it to school—it was kind of girlie—but out here it was okay. He tucked it back down into his jacket. It was cold for

November, but Matt wasn't worried about that. All he could think about was getting to the mail on time.

Usually it took five minutes flat to get to the mailboxes at the top of the road. His mom would be coming home any minute. He needed to get there before her so he could grab the letter he knew was coming. She couldn't see that letter.

"Yip-yip-yip!" he called for more speed.

They were almost at the tall pine tree where he'd be able to see the road. See if there was a red Toyota on it. The dogs sprinted, their feet picking up chunks of ice, which pelted Matt in the face. He crouched on the runners and grinned.

Just as the pine tree came into view, he heard a scream behind him. He whipped his head around to see Bandit, one of the yearlings, racing toward him pulling an empty basket sled. Only it wasn't quite empty. Someone was hanging off the back of it, being dragged along the trail. When Bandit saw Matt and the team, he lowered his head and shot forward. The dog's burst of speed dislodged his passenger.

"Matt!" a voice shrieked. A small figure in a snowsuit tumbled down the trail, rolling like a big blue hot dog.

"Lily!" There wasn't time to yell anything else. Matt

hit the brake on his sled to stop his team. He then threw the snow hook and stomped on it to hold the huskies in place. He prepared to launch himself at the runaway sled. But Bandit crashed into him first, knocking both of them into a snowbank in a pile of legs and fur.

Bandit's eyes, ringed in black—the reason for his name—were full of excitement and chaos. He bounced off Matt and dived for the team, but Matt grabbed his harness. As Matt struggled to hold Bandit, he wondered how his six-year-old sister had managed to harness the young dog with all of his energy and sneak away to follow them.

Lily shuffled toward them, her snowsuit making *sh-sh-sh-sh* noises as she came closer. "I wanted to come!"

"I told you no."

"Bandit didn't like being left neither."

"Not cool, Lily! Bandit hasn't even been trained! What were you thinking? He could've been hurt—" Matt stopped short when he saw his sister's face. Her lip pulled down, her eyes red. "Aw, jeez. Fine! Get in the sled. Just hurry up!"

She stopped crying so fast, Matt knew he'd been played, but there was no time to be mad.

He didn't know what to do with Bandit. Matt was not allowed to take more than four dogs out by himself, and he already had four on the gang line. Bandit leaped and wiggled in Matt's arms. The team grew impatient with the wait. Atlas let out a scream to go.

Matt let Bandit loose and left Lily's sled on the side of the trail to pick up later. There was a fire in his belly now to hurry. Just imagining his mom's face as she opened the letter made him jittery.

Bandit completed a joyous sprint around the team, a goofy grin on his face. And then he took off for home. Foo and Grover immediately turned the team around to chase.

"No!" Matt yelled, but they were already flying down the trail in the wrong direction. So much for listening to him.

"Bandit!" he called, hoping that the dog could hear him above all the pounding feet. Bandit suddenly wheeled around for a crazed drive-by, his mouth wide open in a smile, his tongue flying out to the side of his face. Matt's leaders also wheeled. At last, they were all going toward the mailboxes.

They made it to the big pine, but Matt couldn't even look for his mom. He was too focused on not tipping over as they careened around the corner in a spray of snow.

"Yay!" Lily cheered.

When Matt finally looked up, he sucked in a breath at the sight. It wasn't a red Toyota, but a brown Chevy pick-up, which was almost as bad.

Dad.

By the time the team arrived at the mailboxes, his dad had parked and leaped out of the truck, leaving the door wide open.

"Lily!" he yelled, which was his normal tone for saying anything. "I went to find you in the house, and I didn't know where you were!" He grabbed Lily from the sled and hugged her. "Don't do that again—you scared me!"

The dogs rolled on their backs, making little contented grunts. Matt dropped the snow hook and kicked it in as he tried to figure out how he could get the mail now without his dad noticing. He inched from the sled toward the sixth box in the row.

Lily pointed at him. "We took the dogs out for a ride."

"Yes," Dad bellowed, standing tall. He wore his dusty apron and clogs. "Matthew is taking you whenever he goes out with the dogs now."

Matt froze. "What?"

"I'm too busy with this order, son. I have to get the bowls done on time, or I'll lose the contract. You can look after your sister."

Not for the first time, Matt wished his dad had a normal job. Staying home and making pottery was just another thing for the kids at school to bug Matt about. He also wished he could mention how unfair it was that he had to take Lily all the time. But at the moment, he just wanted to get the letter.

Matt pointed at Lily. "I think she got a bruise from falling off the sled."

When Dad turned to her, Matt lunged for the box with his hand ready with the key. Just as he turned it, the Toyota came around the corner. His mom coming home from her researcher job.

"Aha! A lovely surprise," she said, as she stepped out of the car in her rubber boots and light blue office dress. "Whatcha seen, jellybeans?"

"A purple rhinoceros!" Lily shrieked.

"Good word, Lily!" Mom said.

"Errant children!" Dad boomed.

Matt reached into the box and grabbed the mail.

His mom hooted and came in for a hug that knocked off her orange hat and Matt's ski hat. Nothing Matt's parents did was quiet or small. His mom's frizzy brown hair, always sticking out around her face, tickled Matt's nose.

The large paper flower she wore as a pin on her lumber jacket got crushed between them.

Matt had never noticed how weird his parents were until Jacob had pointed it out when they used to be friends. That was the biggest mistake of Matt's life, letting Jacob come over. He hadn't shut up about Matt's family since.

Matt finally peeked at the mail he was holding. The top letter in the pile had the Sunset School District logo on it. His heart pounded as he read:

To: Clara and Tomas Misco
Box 47 Birch Lane
Copper Creek, MI 48339

"Well, let's all get home," Mom said. "I brought pizza."

Matt was momentarily stunned by this news. They never got cool food like store-bought pizza. But the distraction cost him. Mom reached out like a cobra and plucked the mail from his hands. He watched the letter disappear into her purse.

Two

"What's that, Smokey?" Jacob Tonge asked, hanging over the bus seat in front of Matt.

Jacob's dark hair was plastered to his forehead from wearing a hat, and he had something brown lodged between his front teeth.

Matt could hear others snickering in the back of the bus but didn't turn. "Don't call me that," he said, casually slipping the math assignment into his backpack. Not casually enough, though. Jacob lunged and snatched it out of the bag.

"'Extra-Credit Project,'" Jacob read aloud, as if he hadn't gotten the assignment too. "'Everyone's chance to pull up their grade. Can you still earn extra credit if you can't count?" Jacob grinned as his comment was rewarded with laughter from the back of the bus. He turned back to Matt's homework. "'Create a small business plan,' 'include operating costs,' 'you won't see profits unless . . .' Blah, blah, blah."

Jacob crumpled the paper and tossed it over Matt's head to one of his friends. Matt leaped straight up and caught the ball before Stewart could. Matt might not be good at math, but he was faster than anyone on the bus.

"Sit down in your seats!" Mrs. Wilson yelled. "And face the front!" Her glare burrowed into the wide mirror above the windshield and reflected back to land directly on Matt.

Jacob bumped Matt's shoulder as he clomped past to find his seat. Matt stuffed the math paper into his bag.

"Smokey, Smokey, Smokey." The chant began just as the school bus approached his driveway. The voices followed Matt off the bus. He tucked his neck farther into his coat until the doors closed and the chant was replaced by something else.

Dog song.

Smiling, Matt jogged down the driveway to greet the dogs in the yard and let their howling fill him.

In his room that night, Matt picked up the whittling knife on his desk as he remembered the letter from yesterday. He thought of how Mom had read it and then quietly passed it to Dad. She never did anything quietly. It took her a long time to look at Matt.

"Fighting, Matthew? Really? I can't believe it. Haven't I taught you anything?" She looked as if she was going to cry, which made Matt's throat close up. "I want you to use your *mind,* not your fists."

Why were you fighting? Matt worried she'd ask. He didn't want to tell her what Jacob had said. About "Maniac Misco." That's what the kids called her ever since she'd spoken to his class during career week about being a researcher.

Yesterday his mom had phoned the principal and had learned that Matt was in school on probation. He hadn't been suspended or anything. But when he got home today, she was still looking at him with those disappointed eyes. No big hug. No jellybean greeting.

Matt stared at the poster on his bedroom wall:

ADVICE FROM A SLED DOG:
WORK AS A TEAM
KEEP MOVING FORWARD
HOWL WITH YOUR FRIENDS
BE WARM-HEARTED
LOVE WHAT YOU DO.

The only thing Matt loved about living on a dead-end road with crazy parents and no electricity was the dogs. But it was easy for them to dish out life advice—they didn't have to go to school.

A knot formed in his stomach as he stared at the crumpled sheet outlining the new math assignment.

Extra-Credit Project for the Semester—worth a bonus fifty points to add to your final grade

- Create a small business plan for your idea
- Include operating costs and use formulas to show salary
- Run the actual business for the rest of the semester—six weeks
- Make weekly reports
- You must have at least three clients to show it is a thriving business

You won't see profits unless you have accurate math skills!

What would happen if Matt failed math this year? Everyone would call him stupid, not just Jacob. And his mom . . .

But if Matt could do well on the assignment, it might be enough to bring up his semester average. He was glad there wasn't a letter coming to his parents about his math grade. Yet.

What kind of business could he do? Dad ran his own, but Matt couldn't do his project on pottery. The guys would never let that fly.

Matt picked up his half-finished carving and began to whittle. The head was the fun part. He loved seeing the wood come to life.

Scrape, scrape, scratch, scrape.

Curls of cedar fell from the knife.

He wished math were as easy as whittling. Normally, the way the wood responded to his hands helped him think. But not tonight. Matt put down the knife and opened his glass display case. He ran his fingers over the smooth finished pieces inside, but even that didn't distract his mind.

Matt absently repositioned the carvings, stroking each dog before placing them in front of the little wooden sled. He'd been working on this dog team for almost a year. It was his longest project, and he had to whittle one more husky to make a glorious six-dog team.

Matt's door burst open. His dad's large frame lurched into the room just as Matt closed the display case.

"Homework done?"

Matt slid the math assignment under his books. "Yes, sir."

"Okee dokee. Story. Teeth. Bed." He counted off by smacking his hands together the same way he did every night.

Matt padded into the living room, where he knew most kids had a TV. Lily was already on the couch surrounded by a pile of husky puppies and Pegasus, their mother.

"I'll call this one Boots," Lily said, holding up a black pup with two white front legs. The four-week-old puppy opened her mouth and curled her tongue in a yawn complete with a full-body shake. Pegasus nuzzled the pup worriedly like a good mom. Lily returned the puppy to the pile with her four littermates.

"You only get to name two," their dad said. "So think hard."

"This one's Dragon," Matt said, reaching to run a finger over his favorite. The rusty brown male had a white facemask and fierce red eyebrows. And he howled already, a pebbly sound that made Matt laugh.

"What's it going to be tonight," their mom asked, "Origami Yoda or Marty McGuire?"

Matt didn't know why she bothered asking them both, since Lily always got her way.

"Marty!" Lily yelled.

While his mom read aloud from a book featuring Lily's favorite third-grader, Matt thought of the math assignment. He was lucky Mr. Moffat had given them a chance to make up some marks. Almost as if he'd done it on purpose so Matt wouldn't fail.

School had always been hard for Matt. Gym was his favorite class, but there were no baseball or soccer classes in math. Or dogsledding classes. That's what his school needed.

And just like that, Matt knew what he'd do for his extra-credit project. He jumped up.

His mom stopped reading abruptly.

"I just remembered, I forgot to do my homework."

Dad raised his arms wide in a question. Matt gave him a shrug and ran back to his room.

The propane lamp on the wall hissed as he turned it on and grabbed a fat blue marker and a piece of paper.

He already knew he wouldn't get clients from his school. No one would brave being teased because they'd gone to Smokey's house. He'd have to put up posters at the town library tomorrow morning first thing. That's where everyone put up signs looking for lost cats.

In careful letters across the top of the page, he wrote:

MATT'S SLED DOG SCHOOL

Assignment Report #1

The reports had to be read out loud.

Matt hoped Tammy Fuller couldn't hear his heart racing as she brushed past him on her way to the front of the class. Her blond hair was parted in a straight line and braided in two neat ropes down her back. Green ribbons matched her dress.

Matt hardly paid attention to her as he tried to calm his jitters. His whole body vibrated. *Why do we have to go to the front of the class?* It was bad enough that the extra-credit project had assignment reports that needed to be turned in every week throughout the rest of the semester. Five in total. But now students had to read them out loud. In front of everyone.

"My small business is making all-natural lip-gloss," Tammy began.

She inserted a flash drive into the Smart Board laptop and started up her presentation. "I'm going to mix the ingredients at home, and my mom is going to sell the jars at her store."

Her slide show had charts. *Fancy* charts.

"Here's what's going in the lip-gloss," she said. "I found the recipes online. I put all the oils in the first column—I might not use them all, but I listed the possibilities. The bases are in the second column. You'll notice

Homemade Lip-Gloss by Tammy Fuller

OILS	BASES	EXTRA INGREDIENTS
jojoba oil	shea butter	edible glitter
vitamin E oil	beeswax	cocoa powder
avocado oil		cinnamon
coconut oil		honey
flavoring oils		

I'm using shea butter and beeswax, not Vaseline, because they're better for your lips."

How does she already have charts? Matt wondered.

"I made up seven flavors of lip-gloss. They have delicious names, so they're sure to sell fast! I went ahead and created this pie chart to show which flavors I think will be the best sellers."

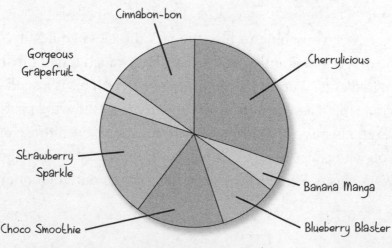

Mr. Moffat smiled. "Thank you for showing us what your business is about. Your charts are very nice. But where are the rest of your answers to our business plan questions from last week?"

Tammy's smug smile faltered.

Mr. Moffat pointed to the list he had taped to the wall next to the door.

BUSINESS PLAN

What is your product or service?
Who will buy it?
What are your operating costs (including your salary)?
How will you attract customers?
What is the competition?
How much will you charge?

"Are you going to buy the jars the gloss comes in?" he asked, still pointing at the list. "How much for all those ingredients? I don't see any numbers here. This is a sixth-grade math assignment. Everyone needs to show the profits and losses calculations we learned about. Even those of you who chose not to start your own business must do the work sheets. Remember, net profit is the amount of money you make minus your expenses. That's the most important number. Next week, okay, Tammy?"

Tammy smiled as if she knew this all along. "Of course."

Mr. Moffat pushed his glasses up with a finger. "Now, who's next?"

Please don't call on me. Please don't call on me, Matt pleaded silently.

"Jacob."

The class listened as Jacob talked about his bottle and can recycling business and how he planned to go door-to-door and pick up people's empty bottles and crushed cans for them. Michigan was the only state in the country to pay ten cents per returned bottle, which was actually a deposit people paid when they bought the bottles in the first place.

"My business is going to take off," Jacob bragged. "Maybe be as big as MotorHeads."

A few students nodded. Everyone knew the Motor-Heads bike shop in town. Even if Jacob's business wouldn't be like a real business, with a product and sales, it was still a great idea. Matt suddenly wished he'd thought of it.

The pounding in his ears grew louder. The room seemed to pulse.

"Matthew," Mr. Moffat said.

Matt's throat went dry. He forced himself to stand on shaky legs and stumbled to the front of the room. All faces turned toward him to stare. His eyeballs froze. Matt wasn't able to do anything but stare back. Someone tittered near the classroom door and it released the spell. Matt clutched his homework sheet in front of him.

"I'm teaching dogsledding," he began.

"What's that, Matthew?" Mr. Moffat said, squinting and leaning toward him. "Speak up."

Matt looked out over the sea of faces and picked a spot on the back wall to stare at. "I'm going to get clients and show them how to run a team. Like piano lessons. But with dogs."

"You're offering piano lessons?" Mr. Moffat asked.

Jacob barked out a laugh.

"*Dogsled* lessons."

"Oh! Well . . . all right, that's a unique service. How are you going to know if your lessons are a success? Will they have to pass a test?"

"Um . . . yeah."

"Sounds interesting. Less mumbling next time, okay? And don't forget the numbers. Now, Chloe Bickle, let's have your report, please."

When the bell rang, Mr. Moffat yelled above the noise of scraping chairs. "Good work, everyone! Nice to see these ideas coming together. I'm looking forward to next week. Matthew, can you see me for a minute?"

Jacob said, "Ooooh!" in a singsong manner as Matt shuffled past him.

After everyone was gone, Mr. Moffat sat on the edge of his desk and removed his glasses. He started cleaning them with his tie, which was never a good sign. "Matthew, I like your business idea."

Matt nodded, not sure where this was going but wishing he were somewhere else.

"I know you've been struggling this semester with the work. I'm glad you've decided to do the assignment and improve your grade. Even so, I'm thinking it might be beneficial for you to get extra help. In the remedial class they do the same type of math but explain it a little more slowly, a little more thoroughly. It might be good for you. I don't want you to fail. What do you think about that idea?"

Matt's throat tightened but he managed to squeak out, "I don't need extra help. I can do better!"

He didn't want to prove Jacob right by taking a special class for kids who needed extra help. What would everyone say? Matt *had* to stay out of the remedial class.

"Okay, then. I'm expecting great things from you in the next few weeks." Mr. Moffatt held his glasses in front of him and peered through.

"Yes sir," Matt said.

"I know you're naturally athletic, so I don't doubt you'll be a great instructor. But you also need to show me your record-keeping skills. Make sure you find three clients so you can calculate your net profits or losses from your gross sales. Just like we've been learning all semester. If you need help accessing the computers, just come to me, okay?"

Matt didn't even remember learning what gross sales were, but they didn't sound good. "Okay," he said, and headed out the door to the buses.

How did *anyone* understand math class? One thing was sure: Matt needed to get started on finding clients before the next report was due.

Three

Just before supper Friday night, the phone rang.

"Matt!" Dad yelled, even though Matt was standing right beside him. "Phone's for you!"

Matt's heart did a little jump of hope as he took the phone. He'd been waiting all week for those words.

"You the one running the sled dog school?" The voice belonged to a boy.

Matt stretched the telephone cord to the limit trying to get out of the kitchen for privacy. He wished again that they had a normal cell phone like everyone else, instead of the old-fashioned landline. But cell phones needed electricity to charge.

"Yup, I'm Matt."

"I'd like to sign up. Can I bring my dog? He's really well trained."

"Um, I guess so. You'd have to keep him away from the sled dogs, though. They don't like pets."

"Okay. We can do that. I'm Tubbs. When can I start?"

"Tubbs?"

"Yeah."

There was a pause on the line before Matt said, "Saturday morning. Classes are on the weekends. Ten bucks a week."

They sorted out the details and times as the dogs began to howl outside. Pegasus and the pups were in the house and immediately tilted their heads, listening. Pegasus threw her head back and let out a long, low howl, which sounded a thousand times louder than normal because it bounced off the kitchen walls.

"What's that noise?" Tubbs asked.

The pups joined in. Their little yodels sounded pathetic next to Pegasus's.

"What *is* that?" Tubbs asked again. "Sounds like you're strangling a cat."

"Nothing. Just be here tomorrow morning," Matt said.

With the dogs howling outside, the pups trying to

sing inside, and Dad's booming laugh, Matt could hardly hear the voice on the phone.

"Gotta go, Tubbs. See you tomorrow."

Lily began to howl with the pups in the corner.

A grin spread across Matt's face. He had his first client.

Matt's Sled Dog School had begun.

❈ ❈ ❈

Saturday morning Matt hurried out of bed and ran along the cold wooden floor of the hall to throw a piece of wood into the wood stove. The kids on the bus complained he smelled like smoke, but that made no sense to him since the stove had a door on it. Still, he wished his family had a normal furnace that blew hot air into the house. Matt hopped from one bare foot to the other as he stuffed the log in and then adjusted the damper on the side of the stovepipe.

At the kitchen sink, he pumped water from the hand pump and set it on the stove for breakfast before he pulled on a pair of wool socks, climbed into his coveralls, and headed to the dog yard. He had a lot of chores to get through before Tubbs arrived.

As Matt crossed the wooden bridge over the creek that ran through their property, frozen now for the season, he wondered what Tubbs would be like. He sounded nice, but that could change once he saw how Matt lived.

The warmth of the barn hit him as he entered. He pumped water into two buckets partially filled with thawing ground chicken parts. The familiar raw smell wafted up as he stirred the contents with an ax handle. Tubbs could meet Matt in the barn. There were only five weekends left until the semester was finished. Matt could call the barn his office, so he wouldn't need to let Tubbs—and hopefully two more clients—into the house.

"You forgot the vitamin pack for Pegasus," Lily said, running up behind Matt as he finished making the dogs' breakfast.

"Don't you have anything better to do?" He took the vitamins from her and stuffed them into his pocket, and then picked up the heavy buckets.

"Dad says you have to watch me, even when you do your sled school thing." Lily put her hands on her hips. "He's working all day, and Mom's got a meeting."

Matt lowered a bucket to hand Lily a shovel. Her smile turned to a pout, but she took it and trudged behind her brother.

As soon as they rounded the corner past the barn, the dog yard erupted with hoots and screams and barks as twenty-two Alaskan huskies ran in hysterical circles, growling at their neighbors. Breakfast time was exciting. Along with snack time, suppertime, play time, and sled-pulling time.

"Calm down, Atlas, I'm coming." As the oldest dog in the yard, Atlas was staked out closest to the house and was the first dog they greeted. The buckets were heavy, and Matt's arms shook as he shuffled quickly to Atlas's circle. It was only a few months ago that Matt had had to stop for a break before he made it to Atlas. Now he noted with pride that he was getting stronger. Carrying buckets twice a day would do that.

Matt was scooping the bloody chicken water into bowls when he heard a vehicle pull up. He turned to see a kid and dog jump out of a gray minivan, which then started backing out of the driveway. Was that Tubbs? So early? Matt hadn't even had breakfast yet.

An enthusiastic yellow Lab dragged a boy about Matt's age toward him. The Lab was all legs and hipbones—a yearling. The boy was the exact opposite. In fact, the closer he came, the more Matt could see the strained look on his full red cheeks, the way his fancy padded coat was clearly too small to contain all of him.

"FLUTE!" Tubbs yelled, trying to stay on his feet behind the dog. Flute saw Matt's dogs now, and Matt could tell this was not going to go well.

Tubbs and Flute thundered toward the footbridge, but at the last minute, the dog veered down the bank instead of staying on the path. Tubbs went down in an explosion of snow. His round eyes were the last things Matt saw before Tubbs disappeared.

A moment later, he saw the Lab slingshot up the side of the creek, dragging a long nylon leash. Tubbs's bright green hat bobbed behind the snowbank as if he was trying to get up but couldn't.

Lily was still staring as the dog flew toward her. She wasn't fast enough to move out of the way. Her arms came up a second before she was mowed down.

"Lily!" Matt dropped the ladle in alarm.

Now the Lab had a clear path to Atlas. The expression on Flute's face told Matt the dog had no sense of self-preservation. He was clearly hoping to make new friends. Couldn't he see the murderous look in Atlas's eyes?

Matt rushed to head off Flute before the Lab reached Atlas. His huskies had turned into a pack, howling for the blood of the newcomer who dared to enter the yard.

"Flute! No!" Tubbs was still rolling around, trying to get out of a hole.

Flute wore a big grin as he lunged to play with Atlas. Matt leaped into the air and tackled Flute just as Atlas's jaws snapped shut behind him.

"Bad dog!" Lily said, standing over them, apparently uninjured.

Flute finally changed his focus and began slobbering over Matt's face. Matt was trying to fend him off as Tubbs shuffled up to take the leash back.

"Holy smoley! You, like, caught him in *midair!*"

"Sled dogs don't like pet dogs," Matt said, trying to keep the pride off his face. It *was* a good catch. "Is this your 'really well trained' dog?"

"Yeah, about that." Tubbs wrapped the leash around his wrist a couple times and bent over his knees as he caught his breath. Matt could hear him wheeze. "Flute needs to finish his obedience training, but my parents . . . they want him to learn too while I'm here."

Matt pointed at Atlas behind him, who was pacing stiff-legged back and forth. "My dogs think he's snack food."

Tubbs sagged a little. Both boys stood a moment, listening to the dogs screaming behind Matt.

Tubbs shuffled. The dejected look on his face made Matt blurt, "Maybe we'll try. Later."

Tubbs immediately brightened. He beamed at Matt. "Thanks! This is going to be great. Flute's a good dog, you'll see. He's just misunderstood."

"For now, let's put him in the pen till the dogs get used to him. They'll be able to see and smell him, but, you know . . . not rip him apart in there."

Tubbs handed Matt the leash, and Matt led Flute to the pen. The dog bounded inside as if he were going to Disneyland. Matt locked the door behind him.

"You may as well help me with chores. I'm not done yet," Matt said, gesturing for Tubbs to follow.

Most likely "Tubbs" is a nickname, Matt thought. But why would you use a nickname like that? Tubbs could have told him his real name, since Matt had never met him.

Another thought occurred to Matt. Tubbs didn't know him either. Tubbs didn't sit on the bus, hadn't heard what the other kids said about him. He hadn't sat in his class and heard him read out loud. Tubbs was here wanting to learn dogsledding. And Matt was good at dogsledding. Matt stood a little taller and led him into the yard.

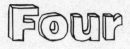

Four

"This is Atlas, my wheel dog. That's the position closest to the sled. He doesn't like pets," Matt repeated, and then glanced at Tubbs. "Obviously."

"Right."

Matt scratched a pure white dog with one blue eye and one brown. The dog immediately snatched his mitten, making Matt wrestle it out of his mouth. "This is Foo. He's smart, so I use him in lead."

"Foo?"

"Yeah—can you tell which dogs Lily named?"

"What?" Lily said, indignant.

"I've got a younger sister too," Tubbs said to Matt,

giving him a knowing look. They nodded at each other, and in that moment, Matt thought maybe they could be friends.

Matt led the way in showing Tubbs the rest of the dog yard. It was a large open space with rows of straw-filled doghouses, each with a sunshade, a sunning platform, and a dog dish attached. Trees surrounded the yard on three sides and the barn ran along the fourth side, with the trail through the woods past that. The breeze blew through the open yard, keeping the bugs at bay during summer.

As Matt introduced the dogs by name and position, Tubbs stood in the middle of the dog yard, looking around and blinking. Matt realized he should have started slower. He forgot sometimes that a full dog yard could be overwhelming if someone was used to having only one dog.

"How can you tell them apart?" Tubbs asked. "They all look the same."

"What? No they don't. Look." Matt pointed to the two sled dogs behind them. "Fester and Arrow are both red, but Fester has a wide face and he always has that impatient expression. See how he looks as if he's about to explode? He just *always* wants to run. Arrow has a pointy face with a calmness in her eyes." It was hard for Matt to believe anyone could think the dogs looked alike.

But the dogs weren't paying much attention to them. Most were focused on the new dog in the pen, shooting him hostile looks. Flute still seemed intent on making friends, gazing back happily.

"I have to use your bathroom," Tubbs said suddenly.

"Just go behind a tree."

"Um . . . no, rather not."

"Well, our bathroom's broken."

"No it's not," said Lily.

"You just got here, man," Matt said. "Seriously?"

"It'll only take a minute." Tubbs shuffled toward the house and Matt had no choice but to follow him. His mind tried to keep up. How was he going to keep Tubbs from going inside their home? Matt hadn't thought this through.

When they got to the porch, Matt stepped in front of Tubbs. "Listen. My parents are different. They have weird ideas about things. Like electricity."

"Electricity?"

"Yeah. They don't believe in it."

"Really? Cool!" Tubbs reached around Matt and grabbed the door handle. "Why not?"

"They used to live in Detroit and decided to go back to nature when they were about to have me. They wanted to live closer to the land or something, so they moved here. Anyway, we don't have running water, so there's no bathroom in here."

That stopped Tubbs. "Where is it?"

Matt reluctantly pointed to the outdoor path leading toward the outhouse, which his dad called the Throne Room. Tubbs peered at the trail but then turned back to the house. Matt quickly tried to think of a way to avoid having Tubbs meet his parents.

Even quicker, Tubbs pulled open the door and stepped in. "Hi!" he called.

Dad peeked his head around a corner and smiled, wiping his hands. He was wearing his bright yellow clogs.

"Hello there!" he said in his loud, normal tone. If Tubbs thought he was being yelled at, he didn't show it. "I'm Matt's dad. You can call me Tom. Who might you be?"

"I'm Tubbs!" Tubbs matched Dad's big voice. "Me and Flute are taking the lessons! That's my dog. We live in town. Holy smoley, it smells good in here!"

Matt stared at Tubbs. He hadn't met anyone besides his parents who was so . . . well, *unquiet*.

"Ah, yes. I spoke with your mom on the phone. Fantastic. Would you like to join us for breakfast? I've just made muffins."

"Sure!"

Matt sighed.

"Matt, show him around while I set another plate."

Dad disappeared into the kitchen, and Matt could do nothing but trail after Tubbs, who was already halfway through the living room. He pointed to the lamps on the wall and turned to Matt questioningly.

"Propane," Matt said.

Tubbs grinned as if this was the best game in the world. He scooted through the living room, paused to hold his hands toward the wood stove, smiled, and then skipped into the wood room. "If you guys live off the grid, why do you have a phone?" he asked.

"Both my parents work. Everyone needs a phone for work. It's also for emergencies."

Tubbs nodded, glanced around, poked at a string of dog booties hanging from the clothesline, and then spotted one of Matt's earlier wood carvings.

"Whoa! Is this a beaver?"

"That's an otter. My mom loves them. I made it for her, but I've made better otters since this one."

"You *made* this?" Tubbs said, incredulous as he ran his hands over the smooth surface. "It looks totally real."

"Except for the part where you thought it was a beaver."

Tubbs grinned and then continued to the kitchen. Matt's mom appeared, dressed for her meeting.

"Well, hello, young man!" She put her hands on her hips and did a quick two-step dance. She ended with her arms open toward Tubbs in a challenge that Matt wasn't sure Tubbs would recognize. Matt cringed, but Tubbs put his hands on his own hips and shuffled his feet in imitation.

Matt stared in shock.

Mom clapped and hooted.

Lily suddenly slammed the door open with her arms full of puppies. The pups were getting more active as they grew older. Once she dumped them onto the floor, they shuffled toward Matt like a herd of manatees.

"I've got to go," Mom said, checking her watch. "You two have fun!"

She opened her arms for Matt to give her a hug. Normally he let his mom be affectionate with him, but right now a hug was the last thing he wanted to do in front of Tubbs.

And just when Matt thought things couldn't get any weirder, Tubbs hugged her instead. There was a moment of surprise on her face before she wrapped her arms around him and laughed.

"Breakfast is served!" Dad called from the dining room.

Mom slipped out as Matt and Tubbs moved to the table. As soon as Tubbs sat down, he grabbed a steaming muffin. He pointed to the bottle of milk on the table as he chewed. "What are those layers?"

"We use powdered milk here. It separates when it's been sitting. It just needs to be mixed," Dad explained, shaking the bottle and pouring some into a glass.

And they drink curdled milk, Jacob's voice was clear in Matt's mind. *It's all chunky and they just stir it and drink it. So gross! Watch out—he's gonna spew chunky milk at you!*

Tubbs shrugged and downed it. "I love milk," he said.

"Well, we're wasting daylight here," Matt said, after draining his own glass. "I've got lessons to get through, Dad. Tubbs, I thought you had to *go?*" Matt gave him a look.

"Oh yeah!" Tubbs stuffed the rest of his muffin into his mouth and waved at Dad as he made for the door. He stopped when he noticed the puppy pile at Lily's feet and bent toward them, but Matt pulled him away.

Tubbs cupped his hands around his mouth and shouted, "Thanks for breakfast, Matt's Dad. I like it here!"

"And we like having you! You come tell me afterward what you learned. Matt, you can find me in the kiln shed. I'm firing today. And take your sister!"

Once they were outside, Tubbs asked in amazement, "Your parents just let you take the dogs out on your own?"

"Sure. They like me doing things on my own. They say they're life lessons. It's called 'free-range kids.' I'm learning about what my skills are."

"I like your parents a lot. I wish I lived like you."

Hearing Tubbs say that did something to Matt's insides. He felt a weird protective pride for his family. To hide his smile, he said, "Are you ready to learn some dogsledding or what?"

"Well, I still have to *go*."

Matt pointed to the outhouse trail, certain Tubbs would take back wishing he lived like Matt's family. But Tubbs laughed, shook his head, and scuttled down the path. When he opened the door and stepped inside, he yelled, "Two holes? There are two holes in here!"

"So? You don't have to use both of them. Just pick one."

Tubbs stuck his head out the door. "*Why* are there two? Is it for, like, emergencies, when you really have to go but someone is already in here, or do you go with your dad or something?"

"Gross! No!"

"Well?"

"'Cause the pile freezes and gets too high, so one hole isn't enough for four people." Matt's face burned. Why did Tubbs ask so many questions?

Tubbs returned after a minute looking as if the whole outhouse experience was the best thing ever.

"Are you ready now?"

"How about we just take the dogs for a walk? You know, for the first lesson. Flute would like that. If you can train him to walk on a leash, that would be great."

"What?" Matt finally realized Tubbs had been stalling. "I thought you wanted to dogsled?"

"My *mom* wants me to learn dogsledding. Translation: she wants me to get skinny." A dark expression crossed Tubbs's face for the first time. "I don't like running."

"Oh. Well, we don't have to do much running. Mostly the dogs do that."

"And she hates Flute," Tubbs rushed on. "She keeps saying he's going to the pound if he doesn't behave. But how can you hate him? He's so funny and smart! So I was hoping you could train him to behave. He's a good dog, really." Tubbs's eyes pleaded with Matt.

Now Matt understood why Tubbs had signed up. Matt's hopes for his math assignment crashed down around him. Tubbs would never pass a dogsledding test if he didn't even want to be there. Matt regretted what he had written at the bottom of his ad poster:

Success or your money back. Guaranteed!

He'd thought that was a clever marketing idea. But what if he ended up having to return Tubbs's ten dollars per week?

And what would that mean for his business if his clients didn't actually learn dogsledding? Matt kicked a hole in the snow. He still needed more clients, and he needed this one to count. Tubbs stood watching him. He looked nervous.

"Okay," Matt finally said. "I think we can help each other."

Tubbs hopped and clapped. "Listening."

"I need three clients to complete this school assignment. If I don't get a great grade on it, I'm going to fail my class. But I don't know anyone else who'll come. If you can help me get two more clients, I'll help with your dog." After knowing Flute for an hour, Matt wasn't at all sure he could train him, but he tried to keep that out of his expression.

"Should be easy enough, then. You have yourself a deal." Tubbs held out his mitten and they shook on it.

Five

"We're taking the dogs for a run today," Matt announced when Tubbs arrived the next day. Tubbs shoved Flute inside the pen and closed the door. Matt didn't know how Tubbs managed to stay on his feet and not rip his tight ski pants as the dog dragged him everywhere.

"Shouldn't we go up and tell your parents where we're going?" Tubbs shuffled toward the house, not waiting for Matt's answer.

Matt chased him. "No snack, though. We don't have time."

"Tubbs!" Dad yelled when they walked in. "Back for more learning?"

Matt's mom smiled. "Whatcha seen, jellybeans?"

"Um . . . a harness?" Tubbs said.

Matt was impressed Tubbs remembered that from yesterday's lesson. *This is a dog harness.* That was about all they'd had time for before Tubbs's mom came to get him. Today Matt was determined to go running.

"Ah! Aren't you clever?" Mom said. She loved when kids got her game and played along.

The way Tubbs planted his hands on his hips, it seemed as if he planned on staying inside for the day.

Dad stood tall, his wiry red hair making him look even taller. He appraised Tubbs critically. "I think you could use some musher clothes. Would you like to borrow these coveralls?"

"They're too long, Dad," Matt said.

"I think we can make do." Dad helped Tubbs into the thick insulated coveralls and rolled up the cuffs twice in two bulky rolls at his ankles. Then Dad picked out a bright scarf and wound it around Tubbs's neck.

"Did you make this?" Tubbs asked Mom, running the scarf through his fingers. "My mom doesn't make things."

"I did," Dad said, stuffing one end of the scarf down the open neck of Tubbs's coveralls. He looked pleased that Tubbs had noticed the scarf was handmade.

A pair of large mitts with braided strings attached were thrown over Tubbs's head and twisted behind his back as if Tubbs were an actual musher. "These are for putting on over your gloves if your hands get cold," Dad explained. "They're attached to you so you can whip them off quickly when you need the dexterity of your fingers, and you won't lose them in the snow. You keep them behind your back like this till you need them, yeah?"

Dad finished the look by pulling an earflap hat snugly onto Tubbs's head. The earflaps stuck straight out like airplane wings. When Dad held up a pair of goggles, Matt shook his head at him, and he dropped them with a sigh.

Tubbs inspected the ridiculously large outfit, then struck a pose as if he were on the back of a sled. "Mush, you dogs!" He beamed and did the little dance that Matt's mom had taught him.

"Mushers don't say 'mush,'" Matt said, just to get him to stop dancing.

"But they knit! I want to learn to knit."

Matt pushed Tubbs out the door. "See you later, Dad. Tubbs is going to learn to scoop poop."

Tubbs stopped in his tracks. "What?"

"First thing you need to learn about dogsledding is what the most important thing is—the dogs. The yard has to be kept clean. Once you take care of that, we're hitting the trail!"

"What about Flute?"

"He'll be okay in the pen for another day. I'll start his training next time." Matt couldn't wait to show Tubbs how the dogs could run. Tubbs was going to love it. He just needed to see what he'd been missing and then he wouldn't want to be inside all the time.

Plus, Matt needed to start actual lessons so Tubbs could pass the test Mr. Moffat had asked about—though Matt still wasn't sure what a dogsledding test would be.

As they cleaned the yard, Tubbs talked nonstop about his new comfy coveralls, and how he thought he might have to go visit the outhouse again but this time he would use the *other* hole, and how he had read last night about alternative power sources, such as using a potato to light a bulb, and wouldn't that be a fun project to try today. Matt reminded him that what they were doing today involved sled dogs and not potatoes.

Tubbs's new earflap hat suddenly went missing, so they had to spend time looking for it. Once they found the hat stashed inside Foo's doghouse, Matt pulled out two sleds and slid them over to the hookup tree in front of the trail. The dogs broke into high-pitched whines and eager screams. Matt smiled and glanced over at Tubbs, but Tubbs was looking as though his breakfast didn't agree with him.

Lily ran out of the house with a slam of the door, her boots pounding over the bridge toward them. "Don't forget me!"

"I'll take the team in front," Matt said to Tubbs. "You can follow and watch what I do. Easy!"

"Okay." Tubbs had become subdued for once.

Matt laid out the gang lines and attached the snow hooks, setting them in their carriers at the back of each sled. Then he explained where Tubbs should position his feet. "You just stand on the runners like this. It's like skiing. See? Not much running."

Tubbs nodded, which Matt assumed meant he understood and was ready to go. Matt sprinted into the barn to grab a bundle of dog harnesses. They were made from different colored webbing and had plush fleece padding on the shoulders. They gave off a bouquet of dog odors.

"Lily, you stay here and help harness. Tubbs and I will get the dogs." Matt handed Tubbs a leash before heading for the yard. The dogs exploded into action. Racing around in circles, they barked and screamed. Matt grabbed his usual leaders and decided to try Fester and Tonka for Tubbs. They were fast young dogs who loved to chase.

"This is going to be so fun," Matt said. "I'm only allowed to take out four dogs on a team when my parents aren't with me. When everyone in my family goes, we take three teams of six dogs."

"You all go out together?"

"Yeah. Sometimes we go out to the base camp and spend the night with the dogs."

Tubbs stared at him. "You camp with your whole family?"

Matt shrugged. It had never occurred to him to question what they did as a family. "It's just what we do. My parents keep the dogs for recreation. The dogs love running, so we take them out as often as we can. But Dad just got a new contract for his pottery, and Mom's busy at work. Since they're not coming, we'll stick with four dogs per team."

He thought he should teach Tubbs how to harness the dogs first, but Matt was too anxious to get started. Plus, the dogs were crazed right now. It would take too long to teach Tubbs.

Matt quickly harnessed the teams himself. The noise level increased as each new dog was added. The dogs clawed at the ground. They spewed foam from their mouths. The dogs who weren't picked screamed their frustration from the yard.

The entire hookup scene was chaos. The air vibrated with the energy pulsing off the dogs. It made Matt jumpy and nervous and excited all at once. He wanted to show Tubbs how much fun sled dogs were. This was the first time he'd gone out with anyone who didn't already know how. Matt's Sled Dog School was about to get real.

Six

Matt jumped onto the runners of Tubbs's sled for a quick demonstration. He figured Tubbs would learn by running a team behind Matt and just watching what he did.

Matt yelled over the noise of the dogs. "Hang on to the handlebar like this." He gripped the wood with both hands.

"Here's your brake." He stepped onto the hinged metal bar at the base of the sled. It pivoted down so the metal teeth dug into the snow. Matt lifted his foot and the brake sprung back.

"Or you can use this." He stepped onto a rectangular

section of rubber tire hanging between the runners of the sled. "It's called a drag. Once you slow the dogs down, you use the snow hook."

He lifted a heavy metal snow hook out of its plastic cradle by the handle and showed Tubbs the two sharp points. "It's your parking brake. You stomp it into the snow like this." Matt demonstrated.

"The more the dogs pull," Matt continued, eager to get going, "the more the hook digs into the snow. It keeps the team stopped. But not for long. You have to watch they don't pop it out." Matt pulled the hook and replaced it.

"Or sometimes none of these work when the dogs really want to go." He grinned. "You can also try yelling, "*Whoa,*" but they won't listen. Got it?"

Tubbs's eyes darted from the barking dogs to Matt, back to the dogs, then to the snow hook. "Okay."

Matt rushed to his sled and then turned around. "And whatever you do"—he yelled to be heard over the dogs' frantic cries—"don't let go! That's the number one rule!"

Matt's skin prickled with nervous energy. He always got butterflies before a run, but today was worse because Tubbs was there. He hoped the trail was hard and the dogs ran fast. He wanted to show Tubbs he was good at this.

Matt waited for Lily to jump into his sled, and then he yanked the snub line attaching them to the hookup tree. The dogs stopped barking immediately, turning their attention to pulling. The sled hurtled forward like a cannonball. Matt glanced over his shoulder to make sure Tubbs followed.

But Tubbs was still staring at the dogs in his team, who were going completely wild with the need to chase.

"Pull the line!" Matt yelled at him. He held up the snub line on his own sled to remind Tubbs what to do.

Tubbs hesitantly reached down and pulled.

The dogs shot ahead and Tubbs barely grabbed the handlebar in time before he was thrown backwards. He didn't let go, but he was off balance.

Matt had most of his weight on the brake. Even so, with all their pent-up energy, his team wouldn't stop— they'd just started.

As Matt watched, Tubbs began tipping sideways. He grabbed frantically at the handlebar but missed and clutched the snow hook instead. When the sled hit a bump, Tubbs dropped the hook and his arms windmilled.

Matt gasped as he watched the disaster unfold. He stiffened in panic when Tubbs performed a spectacular dive off the sled.

What's he doing messing around? Matt couldn't even help him from where he was. Too late, he realized they should have shared a sled.

A spray of snow off the back of Tubbs's sled showed Matt that Tubbs was still connected to it. The loose snow hook had caught the rolled-up cuff on his left leg.

Fester and Tonka had their mouths open wide with deranged glee as they charged toward Matt. All he could see was the bottom of Tubbs's boot as he was dragged by his leg.

Matt heard muffled yelling. Tubbs was reaching for the hook, but all that did was spray a bigger arc of snow. Tubbs's team sprinted about thirty feet behind Matt's team, completely focused on catching up to Matt.

Matt had to concentrate on his own sled for a moment as they whipped around a corner. When he turned back to watch the team behind him, he saw them reach the same corner. Tubbs rolled to the side of the trail as if he were water-skiing behind a jet boat and had been flung out of the wake.

Matt had to do something. Even though his team was still moving, he grabbed his hook and sunk it into the snow. As the dogs ran, the hook carved two ruts into the trail before it snagged on something, stopping them dead.

"Stand on the hook!" Matt yelled at Lily. He didn't have

a second to lose. She climbed out nimbly while Matt prepared to catch the runaway team charging up behind him.

"Whoa!" He grabbed the handlebar of the sled as it
slipped by and jumped on the brake. The team slowed to
a rolling stop. Matt glanced down at Tubbs and cringed.

"You okay?"

Tubbs lay on the trail and groaned.

Matt reached down to pull the hook from Tubbs's
cuff, but it didn't come loose. In Matt's hurry to free it
quickly, the hook caught and twisted in the ripped fabric
of the coveralls.

Without the snow hook to stop them, Fester and
Tonka decided they'd had enough of a rest. They took off
again. Tubbs dragged beside the sled by his leg while Matt,
still holding on to the handlebar, pounded the brake to
slow them down. Lily was still with Matt's team standing
on their snow hook. She yelled at them not to leave her
alone. Matt could hear his dogs going berserk as they faded behind.

"Let go of the hook!" Matt screamed.

"What?" Tubbs screamed back. "Take it! Take the
hook!"

Matt was kneeling on the runners, trying to jerk the

hook loose, when the dogs whipped around the next bend in the trail. He wasn't prepared for the sharp curve and went flying off the sled.

He landed on Tubbs.

This was completely *not* how Matt had pictured their first run.

"Cold!" Tubbs screamed into Matt's ear since Matt was riding right on top of him. Matt took a moment to notice that Tubbs made a good sled.

Tubbs was somehow missing one boot. His white sock stuck out like a beacon pointing the way. Lying face-down on Tubbs, Matt reached across Tubbs's leg and grabbed the snow hook. He leaned all his weight onto it as he planted it into the trail like he had with his own team—even with Tubbs's cuff still attached. The hook sank into the snow and the team jerked to a stop.

Both boys lay there panting. Tubbs had snow packed up his pant legs, filling the coveralls with lumps.

"Am I dead? Did we die?" Tubbs asked.

"Maybe." The snow squeaked underneath Matt as he rolled off.

Tubbs sat up. His face was blotchy red, his nose was running, and his hat was gone. The braided string on his mitts had twisted into a knot, pinning them around his neck. Snow was caked deeply into his dark hair, making it stick up like a snowy crown.

"You passed the first test," Matt said. "You didn't let go."

They looked at each other. A slow grin spread across Tubbs's face.

"You were right about one thing . . ." Tubbs wiggled his sock as if he had just noticed it was missing a boot. "I didn't have to run."

Assignment Report #2

"Since it costs twenty-two cents to make each cup," Destin said, "we'll be making twenty-eight cents of profit with each sale."

Who knew a cocoa stand could do so well?

Destin scribbled out his math on the board.

Expenses:

hot chocolate mix	$13.50
insulated cups (100)	$6.50
mini marshmallows	$2.00
total	$22.00

Cost of each cup of hot chocolate

$22.00 divided by 100 cups = $0.22 per cup

Destin walked proudly back to his seat as Mr. Moffat clapped.

"That's what I'm looking for, people! Before we know how much to charge, we need to know how much it costs to make each unit. Right, Destin?"

Mr. Moffat added to Destin's numbers on the board, his hands moving enthusiastically as if he were a mad composer leading an orchestra.

EXPENSES ÷ UNITS = COST PER UNIT

"Expenses divided by the number of units equals cost," he said, finishing with a flourish. He faced the class with excitement in his eyes.

Matt had started today feeling more confident about his update. He finally had something to report. But now he wished he'd gone first. After listening to Destin's weather forecasts and market survey on the location of his stand, Matt wanted to flee down the hall, exit the school, and go hang with Foo.

Tammy had more charts today, this time comparing flavor experiments for her lip-gloss. And she even brought in sample jars of shimmery goop in all different colors.

"Where are the numbers, Ms. Fuller?" Mr. Moffat asked. "We need to see the rest of the assignment, and that's the costs per unit."

Tammy kept her smile. "That's next week after we start sales, Mr. Moffat. Next week!"

"Hmmm . . . very well. But I'm looking for at least five weeks of tracking expenses—depending on when you actually get started with your sales—by the end of this assignment. Matthew, how has your week gone?"

Matt forced himself to the front of the room.

"Loudly, now." Mr. Moffat nodded encouragingly.

"I got a client," Matt said.

"You got *one* client?" Tammy asked with a smirk. Jen Hunt giggled beside her.

"Mr. Misco," the teacher began. "For this assignment you need at least three clients to be a viable business. Did you follow up with your market research and find ways to advertise to customers? Do you need assistance?"

"No!" Matt said. "I'm getting more clients. I know I need more. But I have one and we've started the lessons."

Mr. Moffat pushed his glasses up and gave Matt a meaningful look. "Do you have numbers?"

"I'm still working on that." Matt glanced over at Tammy. "Next week!"

"Okay, looking forward to it," Mr. Moffat said. "Chloe. Please tell us how your week went with your jewelry-making business."

Matt slumped into his chair. He hoped Tubbs was going to hold up his end of the bargain.

Seven

Tubbs and Matt agreed that they should probably keep the details of their first run to themselves. No need to share them with parents until Tubbs actually found a skill to report about.

"Maybe we should just focus on Flute for a while," Tubbs said over the phone that week. "You said you were going to train him."

"I will. But you have to get back on the horse, so to speak. Next time will be better, I promise." Matt still had no idea how he'd train that dog. And now he wasn't sure he could even train Tubbs. Matt hadn't been expecting someone so uncoordinated to sign up. But it was hard to hold that against Tubbs. He'd gotten dragged down the trail and hadn't even cried. Tubbs was all right.

"Anyway," Matt continued, "*you* said you were going to get me more clients. How's that going?"

Tubbs cleared his throat. "Well, it's been harder than I thought."

Matt tried not to kick the wall in frustration. Instead, he slid down to the floor with the curly phone cord stretched out. Dragon climbed up Matt's leg, his sharp nails digging through the thin material of Matt's pajamas. "Have you tried putting up posters at your school?"

"Huh. That's actually a good idea."

"It would be good if you could do that tomorrow. We've lost a whole week now and I still need two more paying customers. There isn't much time left."

Matt thought about Tammy's pie charts and Destin's cost-per-unit sales numbers and felt as if he were standing on the starting line while everyone else raced ahead.

"I can come over this Wednesday after school. Mom said—" Tubbs was interrupted by screaming in the background. A woman shrieked something about "that idiot dog." Matt heard a crash and Tubbs's voice came out as a whisper. "I gotta go. We can start Flute's training on Wednesday, okay?"

After he hung up, Matt picked up Dragon and pressed his nose into the pup's cheek, smelling his sweet puppy breath. There wasn't any smell better than a puppy.

Matt felt sad for Tubbs. At least Matt's mom was nice—weird, but she didn't shriek at him like that. Or threaten to take the dogs to the pound. She just expected Matt to be smart.

"There you are," Dad said, coming into the kitchen. He clapped his hands together. "Story. Teeth. Bed. Yeah?"

Dragon tripped over himself trying to keep up with Matt on his way to the living room. Lily was already on the couch fitting doll dresses onto the pups. As Matt settled beside them, Boots blinked up at Matt from underneath a wig. Lily held up a book toward Mom.

While his mother read, Matt wondered how he would train Flute while keeping the huskies from picking on him. Matt had to come up with something before Wednesday. He needed a plan. And not just for Flute.

Matt had assumed Tubbs would just copy whatever he did, but clearly Matt needed to teach Tubbs dogsledding step by step. Mushing wasn't something Matt had to think about. Now he struggled to imagine everything he did while running dogs. How did he keep his feet on the runners? How did he steer the sled into a curve? He couldn't remember ever learning how to run, but there was an old picture hanging in the hall of his first Kid 'n' Mutt race, when he ran with only one dog. He needed to start Tubbs with something simple.

And he needed to come up with numbers like Destin had. What were Matt's operating costs? Should he write down what the dogs ate? How much was a sled dog worth?

Mom's voice growled as she imitated a talking bear. Matt directed his attention to her. This was his favorite part of the story.

❀ ❀ ❀

As soon as Tubbs arrived with Flute after school on Wednesday, Matt knew something was up. Tubbs had an unusual expression on his face.

"What?" Matt asked. Did Tubbs want to quit lessons after what had happened on Sunday?

Tubbs's eyes almost disappeared as a smile creased his face. He tugged on Flute's leash. "You were right. The posters worked."

"They did?"

"We got a client. I got a text from someone named Alex who goes to St. Albert School. He heard about my posters and wants to sign up for lessons. He said he had to ask his mom, but then he replied again today. She said yes. He's meeting us here on Saturday!"

Matt slapped Tubbs on the back. "Yes!"

Maybe Matt would complete this project after all. Suddenly the image of having two students falling off sleds came to mind. No, he'd do things differently now. He was the expert and he was going to act like it. Matt raised his chin. His school was growing.

"Now you have to train my dog!" Tubbs stroked Flute's head.

Matt gestured for Tubbs to follow with Flute toward the pen. Time to test his idea.

"Sled dogs don't like pets," Matt said. "It's like they know they're different and they don't trust them. But maybe they just need time to get used to one another."

They locked Flute in the pen and then headed toward Bandit. He was the most outgoing dog from a litter born last year. When Matt released Bandit, the young dog dashed straight to the pen. Bandit stopped to touch noses with Flute.

"They're about the same age," Matt said. "If Bandit likes Flute, maybe the rest of the dogs will too."

As Matt placed his hand on the latch of the pen door,

he glanced at Tubbs, who mirrored Matt's worry. This could get messy. Flashing-teeth, flying-fur, flowing-blood messy.

As soon as Matt opened the door, Bandit dived into the pen with Flute, and Matt sucked in a breath. But then the dogs approached each other cautiously. Matt was surprised, since the last time Flute had bounded toward the dogs as if he'd had a death wish. He must've learned as he'd sat in the pen on other days and watched everyone.

When Bandit bowed down to play, the two began chasing each other up and down the long length of the pen. Tubbs sighed in relief.

"He doesn't seem to care Flute's different," Matt said. "That's a good start."

❈ ❈ ❈

Saturday morning Matt had chores done on time and breakfast over with, even though he felt as knotted up and tangled as a stowed gang line.

"You seem to be taking this project seriously," Dad said. "I'm happy to see you applying yourself to schoolwork."

Matt didn't tell him that this assignment was the most serious thing he'd ever had to do.

Tubbs was the first to arrive. It was as if his mom couldn't get away fast enough every time she dropped him off.

It had been only a few days since Tubbs was last over, but Matt was glad to see him. At school Matt would often smile to himself thinking about Tubbs and his crazy dancing, or his interest in outhouses, or his loud personality.

And he drank their milk.

It made the bus ride home easier.

"Is he here?" Tubbs asked now, shuffling toward Matt. "Alex, the new guy?"

Tubbs sounded worried too, which made Matt feel better. What would the new guy be like? Would he be nice like Tubbs? What if he couldn't hold on to a sled? And what would he say about Matt's family? Would he be like Jacob? Matt wished he didn't need other clients to interrupt his days with Tubbs.

"He's not here yet. You want to put Flute in the pen and I'll get Bandit?"

Before Matt had a chance to unhook Bandit, though, the dogs started the alarm as a black SUV pulled in.

Dad appeared from the kiln shed. He'd been getting ready to fire glazes today and he was already crumpled. Matt wished his dad wore normal clothes. He cringed as his dad strode across the snow in his clogs.

But Matt quickly forgot about Dad when he saw Alex step out of the car.

Alex was a girl.

Eight

The girl was scrawny. She had squinty eyes and shoulder-length dark hair that hung straight from under her hat. She wore a matching ski suit with big boots. Even though she was shorter than everyone there, the way she held her head made Matt feel as if she were looking down her nose at him. Her gaze reminded him of Tammy or Jen, the know-it-all girls in his class who shared looks when he read out loud.

Matt loosened his scarf.

"Hello," Dad said, extending his hand to the woman behind the girl. He realized at the last minute that he was covered in glaze and wiped his fingers hastily on his apron before shaking hands with the tall, thin lady draped in a long fur coat. Matt noticed his dad also had glaze in his hair.

"We're here for the classes," the lady said in a clipped voice. She looked over at Matt the same way the girl had.

"That's my son, Matthew," Dad said in a voice that caused a flock of birds to burst into flight out of a tree. "He's doing a project."

"*He's* running the sled dog lessons?" the lady asked.

"That's right. Your daughter will be in good hands."

"Yes, but . . . he's the one teaching?" the woman asked again dubiously.

"He's been running dogs since he could walk. He knows everything I do. I trust him completely." Dad beamed at Matt with pride, and Matt felt his face start to burn.

The lady stared at Dad for a moment, obviously not sure what to say. Then she turned to the girl. "This is Alexandria."

"Alex," Alex corrected. She looked Matt up and down, and then her gaze moved to Tubbs and on past to the dogs, who were starting to howl. "Mother, I'll be fine. The yard looks just like the ring at riding lessons."

"Alexandria takes English riding lessons, you see— dressage, actually—in the summer. We were looking for something to round out her extracurricular activity for the winter season."

Matt had no idea what dressage was, but by the way the woman spoke, it sounded as if he should be impressed. Tubbs started pretending he was bent over a galloping horse as if in a Western. Matt pressed his mouth tight to stop from laughing.

Alex's mom raised her eyebrows at Tubbs but then ignored him. "I'm Patricia Stevens," she continued. "Extracurricular activity is important to young growing women. Helps them develop to become involved community members. I've been heavily involved with the Young American Girls' Etiquette and Manners Club since its inception, but we've outgrown that now, haven't we, sweetheart?"

"I'm sure that's wonderful," Dad said. "You'd like a kennel tour, yeah?"

Mrs. Stevens looked as if she'd just stepped in puppy poop. She quickly shook her head. "That won't be necessary."

She pulled on her gloves and turned to Alex. "Listen well, dear—you'll need to write everything down later. I'll pick you up at two."

Once she was gone and Dad went back to the kiln shed, Alex marched toward the dogs.

"Well?" she said. "Are we getting started? What's the lesson plan? What are the parameters of success? Do we get a certificate at the end? I heard it's a five-week course and I've missed the first week. I'll have to get caught up."

Matt blinked. "Um . . . yeah, you'll get a certificate."

"Cool!" Tubbs said.

"And there's a test," Matt said.

"There is?" Tubbs asked.

"Excellent," Alex said.

"That's Lily." Matt pointed to his sister, who had just appeared, out of breath. "I'm Matt." He jogged ahead of Alex to lead everyone to the barn.

Lily trailed behind, chattering with Alex. ". . . and you can come see my room, and I'll show you my doll collection, and wait till you see the puppies. How old are you?"

"Eleven and a half," Alex said.

Lily's mitten snaked up to grasp Alex's hand as they walked. Matt was surprised to see Alex smile at his sister. Lily skipped and hummed beside her, swinging their hands.

Matt tried to remember what he'd thought up the night before. Ways to make Tubbs learn better. Ways to understand the dogs. And what did Alex's mom mean that she had to write everything down afterward? Like, everything Matt said?

Pushing away his nerves, Matt introduced the dogs in the yard the same as he had with Tubbs. But Alex didn't look confused like Tubbs had. She looked excited.

"So, why did you pick Foo and Grover as your lead dogs?" Alex asked. "Is it something they're born with? Like how some people naturally have superior intelligence, by genetics or extra study, and become influential?"

Tubbs and Matt glanced at each other in the awkward pause that followed. Foo gave Matt a pointed stare.

"When they're pups, they tell us they want to be leaders," Matt said, noticing with a frown that he'd introduced Foo and Grover at the beginning and Alex still remembered their names. It was clear she wasn't going to forget anything or let anything go.

"But how?"

"They look forward up the trail, like they want to see past the dogs in front of them," Matt explained. "They're brave enough to run in front of the team. They show they're listening to the musher through their bodies. Their ears swivel back, their tails are straight, not held high, stuff like that. Listen, why don't we just start running the dogs. You'll see."

Tubbs went pale. "You sure Alex doesn't want to go inside and see your house first?"

"She can come into my room," Lily said.

"Very sure," Matt said.

"Can I be on your sled?" Tubbs asked.

"Good idea," Matt said. "Alex can follow behind and watch us." As soon as Matt suggested this, he realized that was exactly how he'd tried to teach Tubbs. But the thought of Alex dragging by her pant leg and screaming was strangely comforting.

Tubbs immediately relaxed and then shared a look with Matt, clearly remembering what can happen to the person following behind.

"That's your idea of a lesson?" Alex asked with a tone of voice that was already so irritating, Matt hoped he didn't hear it in his sleep.

"We'll go slow, for all the people here who weren't born with superior intelligence," Matt responded.

Alex stared at Matt, bristling. Matt stared back. Their stares turned into a challenge, both trying to make the other break eye contact first, like two dominant dogs.

Nine

Lily was the one who broke the war of wills. "I can go with Alex! I can help her," she said, tugging Matt's arm.

He frowned, not wanting to see in his mind Lily dragging down the trail with Alex. But if Tubbs was coming with him, it made sense for Lily to go with Alex. She *could* actually help. She knew more than the two students.

"Okay. But we'll just hook up three dogs for you guys." The chase team wouldn't need as much power since they'd be so focused on catching up to the team ahead of them. The dogs would pull harder, and they'd have less weight to pull with just the two girls.

Back at the barn, Matt hauled out two sleds again. The dogs started up their screaming. Matt watched from the corner of his eye as Alex took in the whole scene with a look of complete confidence.

After Matt prepared the sleds, he collected Grover. If Alex wanted lessons, he would fill her head with so many facts that she wouldn't be able to remember them all, let alone write them down. Whatever she was doing that for.

"See this harness?" Matt held it up and folded it in half. "You fold the part with the double webbing and it makes two holes. Then you slip it on over the head like this." He slid the harness over Grover's sleek head. The dog helpfully lifted a paw, eager to be going. Matt glanced at Alex to see if she was impressed with how smart his dog was.

"Then you hook the back of Grover's harness to the tug line. It's attached to the gang line. The gang line is attached to the sled, so when the dogs pull, they all put their power into moving forward, and that moves the sled forward. We'll hook up a few more."

Matt hooked Foo beside Grover. "We have more leaders, but I like using these dogs because they run well for me. We have a connection."

Matt stroked Foo's bristled white muzzle. The dog's multicolored eyes glanced up at him innocently and then, in a flash, snatched the large mitt that Tubbs wore dangling on its string.

"Hey!" Tubbs said, pulling on his string. "Mischievous white beast!"

Matt rescued the mitt, grinning. He felt as if he'd grown up with these dogs. He used to sneak out to their pen to sleep with them when they were puppies. Foo would drape his fat body across the warmth of Matt's neck and fit perfectly. When Matt was learning to run his own team, the yearlings were learning to pull. And Matt would spend hours just being out with them in the dog yard, or having entire conversations with Foo. Matt had run them so often now, he thought they even preferred to run with him rather than Dad. Sometimes Foo knew which way Matt planned to go before he even told him, as if the dog could read his mind.

"Atlas is the wheel dog—that's the dog closest to the sled. It's usually a strong dog. Sometimes wheel dogs have to slam their tugs to get the sled unstuck. It's called popping the tug. The leaders are the smart ones. They know the commands—'gee' and 'haw.' Some other commands are 'gee over,' 'haw over,' 'come around,' 'on by,' 'trail,' 'hike up,' and 'whoa.' Get it?" Alex only nodded.

After they hooked up three dogs for Alex's sled, Matt went over the brakes with her. He showed her the snub line, how it attached the sled to the tree, and how she needed to yank the half-hitch knot to release the team and follow him.

Alex looked down her nose at him. It was a long pointy nose, like the kind Matt saw on witches in fairy tales.

"What do I do next?" Alex asked.

She'd never even done this before, so why was she looking all know-it-all? Maybe that was her expression all the time, Matt thought. Or maybe she was as scared as Tubbs and hid it better.

"Stand on the runners and hang on. It's going to be crazy. Do *not* let go. That's rule number one. If you fall off, we can't go back for you."

Lily climbed into the basket of Alex's sled, all smiles and completely trusting. Matt had a moment of regret and wished he'd told Lily to go in his sled. But that would look dumb now. And it wasn't as if Lily hadn't done this before. So Matt jogged to his sled and motioned for Tubbs.

"I'll stand on this runner and you stand on the other runner, and hold on to the handlebar of the sled like this." Matt used both hands to show him.

The noise of the dogs at hookup always got Matt's heart pumping, but it appeared to terrorize Tubbs. The whites of his eyes flashed, and he was breathing so fast, Matt worried he'd pass out.

"Don't worry," Matt told him quietly. "I won't let you get dragged today."

Matt could tell Tubbs was trying to be brave. The large boy thrust his shoulders back and stepped onto his runner. The earflaps on his hat stuck straight out and fluttered slightly with the movement.

Matt pulled the snub line attaching them to the tree and called to the dogs. "Ready? All right!"

The dogs blasted ahead just as Matt reached an arm around Tubbs so he wouldn't fall backwards. Matt glanced behind to see Alex pull the snub, cling to the sled like a monkey, and whip out of the yard after them with a huge grin on her face.

"Cowabunga!" She laughed into the wind. The loose hair around her hat slapped her face.

They didn't get far down the trail before it became apparent that Tubbs wasn't going to stay on his runner. Matt had to keep grabbing him and holding him, plus watch his team, plus watch the dogs behind him to make sure they weren't going to get hurt, plus make sure his sister was safe.

Matt signaled to Alex to use her brake as he slowed his team and turned to Tubbs. "Do you want to ride in the sled? Your only job will be to jump out if we need to untangle dogs, okay?"

Tubbs practically dived into the toboggan sled. It was fitted with a coated nylon sled bag. Tubbs planted his butt and gripped the sides of the sled bag tightly. It came up to his chest. They took off again. Foo and Grover's shoulders rubbed against each other as they matched strides and pounded around the next bend. As he always did, Matt felt a fierce pride watching them work. The joy that radiated off the dogs clung to him too.

When the sled skidded around the corner, Matt stuck his foot out for balance. He hung his other heel off the runner to dig into the trail to carve a tighter turn. These were the types of things he did that were hard to explain. He didn't even know he was doing half of them until he paid attention because someone was behind him watching.

Matt glanced back to see Alex do the corner perfectly. She leaned in and stuck out a foot. The sled skidded with a rooster tail. Matt heard Lily hooting in the basket.

Even if Alex weren't a girl, Matt still didn't think he'd like her.

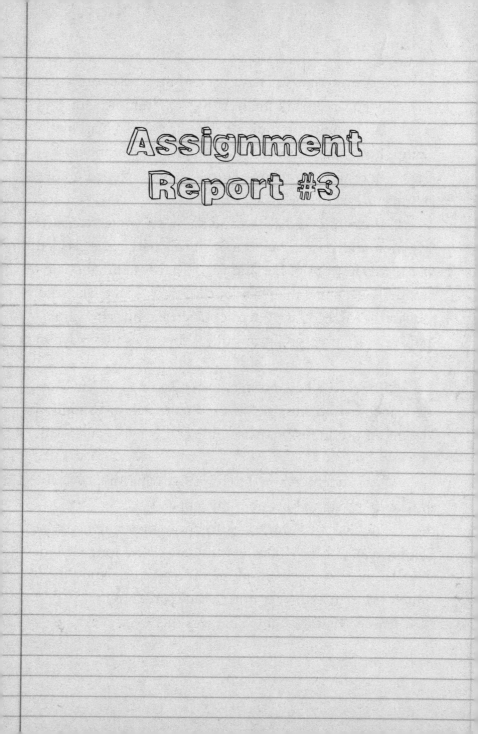

Assignment Report #3

"And now that we have a customer base, our sales will only go up during the next weeks," Tammy said. She used a laser pointer to indicate the numbers in her Power-Point show. Matt couldn't understand her numbers because there were so many zeros. And who owned a laser pointer?

"I thought I'd go ahead and show my projected sales. My mom didn't even help me with this part." She clasped her hands in front of her and gave Mr. Moffat that syrupy teacher's-pet smile that everyone knew was fake fake fake, except for Mr. Moffat. "I predict Cherrylicious and Cinnabon-bon are even going to outsell the gloss they have in the mall."

"'Projected sales' doesn't mean guessing . . ." Mr. Moffat leaned in and squinted at the Smart Board. "A million dollars of product sold, Miss Fuller? Let's just stick with the exercise."

Matt suddenly wanted to high-five Mr. Moffat. Maybe he did know something about teacher's pets.

"The task this week was to show how much you're getting paid," Mr. Moffat continued. "How long does it take to make a jar of lip-gloss? You need to know how much you're making per hour at any job, correct?"

Uh-oh, Matt thought. That was this week's task?

"People, please have your salary—that's how much you are making—figured into your numbers. Next: Jacob, what do you have for us?"

Jacob sauntered to the front. "I've made a financial report." He held up some papers he'd taped together to make one long piece.

"Here's my balance sheet of operating costs. It was simple to make if you know how to count." Jacob smirked at Matt. "I think my business is the best because I'm making thirty-five bucks an hour and I've only just started! I bet even MotorHeads doesn't make that much. I'll be a billionaire before any of you losers!"

Bottle and Can Recycling Service by Jacob Tonge

Assets:
milk crates to carry bottles
long toboggan to go door-to-door of neighborhood
Dad's truck

Expenses:
fuel to drive to depot center $7

Total time to do pick ups
1 hour

<u>Sales (5 clients)</u>

Kruegers	$13.00
Smiths	$8.00
Makis	$5.50
Schultzs	$9.00
Lewises	<u>$6.50</u>
total	$42.00

	Debit	Credit
Income		$42
Expenses	$7	
Total	$7	$42
Net Income		$35

Mr. Moffat sighed. "What about the cost of the vehicle and driver? I know you do the pickups on your own, but you need to rent the truck from your dad to take all the bottles to the depot. That goes down as an expense, same as paying your employees. Unless you're driving yourself?"

The class laughed and Matt felt a bit better.

"The expense of the driver and truck will bring down your net profit. And how long does it take to return the bottles? That will add time to your hour of work." Mr. Moffatt pointed to Jacob's chart.

"Even with those extra expenses, you've got an impressive net income! But don't forget, this is a longer-term project. How many clients will you have next week? Since bottle returns aren't a weekly occurrence, you'll have to calculate your average salary at the end. But great job so far!"

Jacob bowed before walking back to his desk, making everyone laugh. "Millionaire walking, yo. Make room."

"Matthew!"

Matt sat up straight.

"Let's hear how the dogsledding business is going." Mr. Moffat looked at him expectantly. "This is week three. You should all have solid numbers and be half-done on your reports."

Matt's face felt hot as he slid out of his seat and went to the front. He didn't have any numbers yet. He didn't have balance sheets or charts or any figures. He'd been so busy just trying to deal with the clients he had.

"I have two paying clients now." Matt looked down at his feet.

"Excellent! That's double your sales of last week," Mr. Moffat said.

Matt looked up with surprise.

"What's the percentage?" his teacher asked.

When Matt stared at him blankly, Mr. Moffat explained himself. "You had one, now you have two. Double the sales. What percentage of growth is that?"

"Fifty?" Matt guessed.

"In business it's called one-hundred-percent growth! Nicely done. Now make sure you get three paying customers and then you'll have enough revenue to work on your balance sheet. Next week."

Matt nodded.

"And how are the lessons going?"

"Um, good. I have . . . a lesson plan and . . . parameters of success."

Mr. Moffat's eyes widened a fraction before he smiled and pushed up his glasses. "That sounds fabulous. Now, Destin. Let's see what you've got."

Confused but relieved, Matt scurried back to his chair. One more client and then he may be able to pass this assignment and class after all. But he really needed to figure out first what a balance sheet was.

Ten

"**H**ow's your business coming along, Smokey?" Jacob asked as he knocked Matt's hat off from behind. Jacob was smart enough to stay in his seat as Mrs. Wilson eyed them in the rearview mirror. "Doesn't seem like you have your numbers figured out. I've got a question. How many dummies does it take to screw in a light bulb?" He said it loudly enough that the whole back of the bus paused to hear the response.

Squeezing his eyes shut, Matt thought he knew what was coming. He didn't turn around.

"Oh, wait a minute. There *are* no light bulbs in Smokey's house. They use dog farts to light up the room."

A few kids burst out laughing. "They have pretend electricity, like pretend flowers, right, Smokey?"

Matt's stomach tightened. Normally he hid the paper flower his mom made him every day and put into his lunch. She'd been doing it since he started school, and he didn't want to hurt her feelings by telling her he was too old now. Today, he hadn't gotten rid of the flower fast enough before Jacob had seen it.

Jacob tried to keep his audience, but conversations started back up. He settled into the seat behind Matt.

Matt stared out the window and considered how he could ride with Lily to school instead. Her little bus went right past his school on the way to hers. But then Jacob would *really* have something to say about him.

As the power lines whipped past, Matt imagined what it would be like to take the dogs to school, running the ditches beside the road as the bus drove by. Everyone would see him running sled dogs and forget his family didn't have electricity.

Matt sighed. As if they would ever think running dogs was cool.

❄ ❄ ❄

Scrape, scrape, scratch, scrape.

In his room before supper, Matt whittled the ears of the sixth sled dog and stewed over perfect Alex. She hadn't fallen off once during the whole run on Saturday. Even Tubbs wouldn't stop talking about her. She was smart, too. How could she be good at everything?

Sh-sh, sh-sh, sh-sh.

Even sanding the carving couldn't calm his mind. Matt needed a lesson plan before the weekend. Something big to challenge Alex and her perfect skills. He placed the half-finished dog on his desk and went to find Dad.

Dad raised his head from the pottery wheel when Matt entered the workshop. His father had been in the kiln shed every evening firing, and now he was back in his workshop making more pottery. The spinning clay on the wheel slowly came to a halt as he stopped the pedal.

"Son, can you wait a minute? I'm almost done with the last of this set of bowls."

Good, thought Matt. *He's distracted.* "I just have to ask a quick question. For this weekend's lessons, I'm thinking of using one team so I can explain things easier to Tubbs and Alex. But if I still have to take Lily, that's four of us."

"You still have to take Lily."

"We'll need more than four dogs. Can I hook up a bigger team, just this time?"

Dad looked thoughtful for a moment. "That's good logic. With the extra weight you'll have, you can hook up who you need. Watch Gem—she's in heat."

"I know that."

"Right. Don't take her—liable to have a fight on your hands. And leave Banjo, too. His attitude's been down lately. He needs some time off."

"I noticed that. But I don't need him, either."

"Good, then. Do what you think is best. I know you'll take care of those dogs. I'm impressed you're running things while your mom and I are so busy lately. You're doing a great job. Soon as I'm done with this big contract, we'll all go together again, yeah?"

"Sure. Oh, I've got one more question. What are the operating costs for running the dogs?"

Dad blinked at Matt. "Your school project, right? Let's see, we've got vet bills, the sleds and equipment." He used his fingers coated with slick gray clay to count off. "The gear for the musher—though I suppose you put all that down as assets, right? Stuff we already own. Have you learned about that? Of course you have. So, expenses mainly would be the dog food. Let me think . . . haven't recorded it—it's just something that we have to buy. Worth it, though. Can't put a price on quality of life. Do what you love . . ."

"Love what you do," Matt responded, as he always did. It was their family's favorite dog wisdom quote.

"So, with the bags of quality kibble," Dad continued, "the packets of vitamins and minerals, the chicken fat, the rice, and the ground meat slabs, I'll guess it's about twenty bucks a month per dog."

He bent his head to his work and started with the clay again. Matt was about to escape when the wheel stopped a second time and his dad asked, "How are your students coming along?"

Matt sighed. "Tubbs can't figure it out, but Alex seems to know everything already. Like, everything in the world."

"Ah, yes. Alex. Well, no matter how much you know, somewhere, someone is going to be better than you."

"But dogsledding is usually what *I'm* better at."

"You're still better at it than she is. She's only just learning. And you're maybe a bit less abrasive with others. Everyone likes you. Do you think sometimes it's more important to be kind to people than to be better?"

Matt nodded and slipped out, thinking about when he'd gotten into that fight with Jacob. The way some of the kids on the bus called him Smokey. Some even laughed and pretended to bump into him in the halls. Matt didn't tell Dad that people didn't seem to like him, either.

Eleven

Matt glanced at his notes from the night before, thankful that he had made them now that Alex stood in front of him with her hands on her hips and an expectant look in her eyes. Something about her made him forget what he was going to say.

Foo   Grover
Fester   Tonka
Savage
Atlas   Arrow

Matt looked over the sled tied to the hookup tree. His eyes roamed the long gang line laid out and then surveyed the dog yard. When his gaze landed on Foo, Matt let out a tiny breath. The dog caught his eye and wagged his tail as if he knew what Matt had planned and liked it.

Tubbs peered dubiously over Matt's shoulder. "Thought we weren't taking more than four? And why is there a big space there?" He pointed to the empty spot on the sheet where no dog was listed.

"We're all going together today," Matt said, on his way to the barn. "One sled. You and I will sit in the basket, and we'll let Alex run the team."

Tubbs and Alex followed as Matt talked. He snuck a glance at Alex expecting terror, but he saw only excitement in her eyes.

"It's good to have an empty space on the gang line, in case we have to move dogs around," Matt continued. He opened the food bin and noticed with annoyance there weren't any chicken chunks cut. "Also, we don't need eight dogs."

Matt's chest tightened thinking about running even *seven* dogs. So much power. Anything could go wrong. He had a moment of doubt about his plan. Should he really take seven?

He slid out a fifty-pound block of frozen ground chicken and ran a hacksaw over the top to mark where it needed to be cut. "So like I said last week, all the positions on the gang line have a job. The leaders will be the smart ones. Foo and Grover always listen to me." He recalled a certain run to the mailbox—when they had turned around to chase Bandit—and corrected himself. "Except when they don't."

"What is that stuff?" Tubbs aimed a finger at the frozen block.

"Dog snacks." Matt swung the ax, chopping along the lines he'd marked to cut chunks of ground chicken roughly two pounds each. This reminded him that he still needed to figure out all his operating costs.

"Next are the point dogs," Matt continued as he chopped. "Or they're sometimes called swing dogs."

"You're cutting pieces for all the dogs in the yard," Tubbs pointed out.

Matt paused and shrugged. "So?"

"That's twenty-two pieces and they're all exactly the same size. You didn't even stop to think about it. If I could do that, it would make me irrationally happy."

"Everything makes you irrationally happy!"

They grinned at each other.

"I do this all the time, so it's not that hard," Matt said. "Anyway, we'll use Fester and Tonka in point. The dogs you had in lead before." Matt wasn't sure about taking Fester, but he didn't have the heart to leave him behind.

"The insane ones," Tubbs observed.

"That's them," Matt said. "Point dogs are like leaders in training. They watch the lead dogs and learn which way they're supposed to go when I shout 'gee' or 'haw.'"

Alex nodded and, to Matt's dismay, took notes on a little pad.

"What are you doing?" Matt asked.

She looked up. "Trying to learn. I plan on becoming a musher at the end of these lessons. I'm going to train my collie at home."

Of course she was.

"So am I!" Tubbs did a little happy dance, his fascination with the frozen chicken forgotten. He wore coveralls, the new hems from where Matt's dad had shortened the length hanging over his boots and almost meeting the snow.

Dad had decided to give him the set of coveralls last week, but Matt wasn't sure if his dad somehow knew about the cuff incident or if it was just a coincidence that he'd cut the pants to fit Tubbs. Matt stared at the cuffs for a moment as an idea hit him. Coveralls could be an operating expense! He just needed to find out how much they cost.

He suddenly felt better about his next assignment report. Thank goodness for Tubbs and his cuffs.

"After the point dogs are the team dogs," Matt continued, as he loaded a burlap sack with seven chicken snacks. "Their only job is to pull. They're just happy to be there. Savage is in team position." Matt dumped the rest of the chunks into the storage bin.

"Last are the wheel dogs, closest to the sled. They're the strongest in the team. Atlas and Arrow are the muscle today." Matt stuffed the burlap sack into the sled bag. "Okay, let's harness 'em and go!" Hookup took several minutes, but finally they were ready.

In the chaos of barking and screaming dogs, Matt approached his sister.

"You have to stay here, Lil. There's no room in the sled." Matt didn't want her getting hurt. The best place for her was at home.

"That's not fair!" she wailed.

"We won't be long. You clean up the yard, and by the time you're done, we'll be back."

Matt felt only a slight twinge of guilt as he prepared to leave her in the yard. There really wasn't room in the sled with Tubbs along.

Tubbs wedged himself in first on top of the chicken.

Matt jumped in next. When he caught Alex's expression, he finally saw fear on her face as she stepped onto the runners and looked down the gang line at the long line of dogs leaping and frothing in front of her.

"Ready?" Matt called to the dogs. Foo glanced over his shoulder at him, eyes sparking. Matt could almost hear Foo telling him he was ready and able to lead this long string of dogs. "All right!"

The team whipped out of the yard so fast, it captured Matt's full attention. This was a powerful team.

Foo and Grover set a blistering pace. All the dogs galloped until Matt told Alex to step on the rubber drag. It forced the team to shift down to a trot.

"This. Is. Awesome!" Alex's eyes shone.

When they reached the fork in the trail, the path on the left would take them to the mailboxes. But today they were going on a longer run.

"Gee!" Matt called. He proudly watched his leaders swerve to the right and fly down the trail without hesitation.

Atlas started wobbling. When Matt saw his tail rise, he knew what would happen next.

"Tubbs!" Matt yelled. "Keep your mouth closed!"

"What?" Tubbs turned to Matt just as Atlas started

to poop. With their speed, the nuggets bounced off the ground and launched toward the boys.

"Augghhhh!" Tubbs put both arms out in front of his face in horror. Then he must have realized that Matt's advice was wise, because he clamped his mouth shut with a mitten.

Matt had no time to respond as they whipped around a corner. The sled leaned precariously on one runner.

"Lean out!" Matt yelled at Alex, pointing to the left.

Alex leaned her body as if she'd done so a million times. She pulled the sled back onto both runners. Snow flew up behind them.

Alex's whole face glowed with joy. "Just like skiing!" she yelled. "I'm ranked number one on my ski team."

Why am I not surprised? thought Matt.

Finally, the dogs started to settle, everyone in trotting mode again.

"What's wrong with that dog?" Alex asked, pointing.

Matt knew she was talking about Savage.

"Is he limping?" she questioned.

"No, he's pacing. That's how he runs normally. His front foot and back foot move at the same time on the same side. Most dogs switch to pacing if they're getting tired. It's just a different way of running. That's how I know it might be time to put them in the basket or take a break. But if Savage starts normal trotting, instead of pacing, then I know he's getting tired."

Savage twitched his ears hearing his name but stayed focused on the trail ahead and continued pulling. Matt felt a tightness in his chest watching Savage keep his tug line tight. They were such honest dogs, and they continually amazed Matt with what they could do.

"Wow. So you have to know each dog really well, then."

"Of course I know my dogs well! That's what mushers do."

It took them a record twenty minutes to get all the way to the base camp. Normally it was a thirty-minute run. This was the area where Matt's family set up their prospector tent for when they wanted to camp overnight. They could go out on different trails from here. The dogs knew this was a rest stop, so they dived into the snow as soon as Matt called a halt. They rolled on their bellies, cooling in the snow, biting mouthfuls. Fester glanced back at Matt, frost covering his muzzle, a contented expression on his face at last. That dog seriously lived for running.

Alex hopped off the runners, leaving the sled as if it were a bike leaning against a tree.

"Wait! The hook!" Panic made Matt flail. He was stuck in the sled. "You forgot—Tubbs, get off me, man!"

He needed to sink the snow hook into the ground before the dogs decided to take off again. Matt fumbled in his hurry to get past Tubbs. Their legs tangled. Tubbs fell sideways onto Matt and they both tumbled out of the sled in a heap. Matt jumped up, grabbed the hook, and stomped on it.

"Never leave the sled without setting the hook!" Matt screamed at a surprised Alex. His blood roared past his ears. "So many dogs! Do you know what could have happened if they had taken off?"

Matt couldn't stop the visions of the team running without a driver on the brake. Dogs tripping, getting dragged, sprained shoulders, tangles, fights. The dogs trusted him to keep them safe. His fear at what nearly happened turned into anger directed at Alex. She and Tubbs stared at him.

"You think you know how to do everything perfectly with all your note-taking? You could have hurt the dogs! What kind of student does that?"

Alex narrowed her eyes and raised her chin. "I remember everything you've said to me, and you've certainly never said that before. Rule number one: *don't let go*. But you never mentioned rule number two is to *always set the hook*." She poked a finger at him. "When students don't learn, it's the teacher's fault. Everyone knows that. There aren't any bad students, only bad teachers."

Matt gaped at her with nostrils flared. His heart flipped as her words sank in. He was a bad student *and* a bad teacher.

The moment was broken by the dogs. As one, they stopped rolling and turned to stare at the trail where it came out from the forest. Their ears perked forward.

And that's when Bandit broke out of the trees. He flew toward them, tongue out, a satisfied expression on his face as if he'd been tracking the team for a while and was proud he'd found them.

He was pulling an empty sled.

When he spotted Matt, he grinned even wider. Matt threw out his arms to fend off the young dog as he leaped.

"Bandit? What . . . ?" Matt suddenly realized what the empty sled meant. Dread hit him like a snowball.

Lily.

Twelve

"Bandit, what are you doing here?" But Matt knew what the dog was doing there. He thought back to the route they had taken. There were dozens of corners, dozens of places where a musher could have been thrown off. Lily could be at any of them. And she could be hurt.

Foo lay flat, his chin resting on the snow between his paws, his eyes following Matt, as if he could feel Matt's distress.

"I have to go," Matt said.

"You're leaving us here?" Alex asked.

"My sister fell off this sled somewhere. I have to get her."

"We can come help," Tubbs said.

"Yes, let us help," Alex said, their fight suddenly forgotten. She looked as worried as Matt.

"Okay," Matt said. "But we have to hurry. No time to snack the dogs. Let's turn the team around."

After a moment's hesitation, Matt hooked Bandit into the spare place in the team beside Savage. This wasn't how Bandit's first real run with a full team should happen, but at least it was a good spot on the gang line where Matt could keep an eye on him. Not too close to the front or to the sled, where he could be easily scared. And he'd already had his first two runs with Lily. It was a mystery to Matt why she kept choosing Bandit out of all the dogs in the kennel. Why an untrained yearling? It didn't matter now. He had to find her.

"I'm driving," Matt said to Alex.

She nodded and climbed into the sled with Tubbs.

"Ready? All right!"

When they took off, Bandit looked around as if he couldn't believe he was part of the team. Then he felt the pull on his tug line. He put his head down and charged with all the passion of a yearling. Savage glanced at him with a knowing look. The older dogs had the experience to know how to pace themselves. Bandit would learn.

Soon they arrived at a T-intersection where they'd

done a hard gee. Lily could have fallen off here. Matt stopped the team and kicked in the snow hook.

"Lily!" he called, cupping his hands around his mouth.

The dogs watched him strangely over their backs. Matt felt their eyes on him, felt their unease at his panic. But he knew they trusted that he would get them out of whatever situation this was.

"Lily!"

They all paused and listened.

Nothing. No sounds but the chatter of a squirrel and the trees rubbing together in the breeze. Melting snow plopped off branches. Lily was not here. Matt jumped back onto the runners.

"Where is she?" Alex asked, obviously aware of the danger Lily was in. Her eyes met Matt's and he shook his head.

At the next corner, Matt was sure he'd find Lily lying on the trail, knocked unconscious from hitting a tree. He peered at the solid pines and spruces lining the route. The trees appeared dark and angry, their branches morphing into frowns. She wasn't here, either.

Each time they stopped, Matt called her name. When there was no response, he imagined worse things. He wasn't alone.

"What could've happened to her?" Tubbs asked.

"What if she dislocated an arm?" Alex said. "Or could she have flown off the sled and broken a leg?"

"I don't know," Matt said.

"Maybe she poked an eye out," Tubbs said, before Alex nudged him quiet.

Matt scanned the sharp willows that grew along the side of the trail. He shuddered to think of his poor sister maimed for life all because he was too busy trying to prove he was better than Alex. He hadn't watched Lily like he'd said he would. He'd never let her down before. Sometimes he wished his parents didn't believe in free-range kids. It was too stressful.

The dogs ran faster on the slick trail. Matt kept on the drag to slow them down so Bandit wouldn't be nervous about the speed. He also needed time to look around.

"Can I help with the team somehow?" Alex asked.

Matt shook his head. "Just be ready to jump out if I ask you to grab a dog. This is a huge team. It's hard to control them plus look for Lily at the same time."

Matt didn't tell her that he'd run this many dogs only with Dad on the runners with him. Why had he made Alex run them? He'd put the dogs in danger and they trusted him to keep them safe. Alex didn't even know enough to be scared. And why had he left Lily?

They followed the route back along the same humps and dips and turns. Past the spot where Tubbs had elbowed him in the ribs, on by the place where Fester had also pooped on the run. They slid over the mess, leaving smears in the snow behind them.

They kept running. Each time they arrived at a new twist in the trail, Matt stopped the team and everyone listened.

"Lily!" Matt called desperately. He gripped the handlebar tighter with each passing minute.

On the last stretch of trail before home, the dogs broke into a lope. This was where Matt usually told the team to go faster. The dogs were used to the routine.

Bandit ran with abandon, his legs flying out in all directions. He glanced over his shoulder at Matt, seeming to check that he was doing well. His tail rose in hesitation.

"You're okay, Bandit. You're safe," Matt assured him.

Bandit straightened out his tail again and continued pulling.

"At least we haven't seen her lying on the trail," Alex said. "If she's not out here, that must mean she went home."

Matt forced himself to breathe. Alex was right. That's where Lily would be, back in the dog yard where he'd left her. She might even try to pretend she hadn't come after them—what with her wiping out and losing Bandit. She was probably worried she'd be in trouble. And when Matt got his hands on her, she would be.

They broke through the trees and into the yard. The rest of the dogs started a welcome howl. Matt stopped in front of the barn and sank the hook. He jumped off the runners and ran straight into the barn.

"Lily!" he called. "Lil?"

It took a while for the three of them to search through the barn and kiln shed and inside the house before they realized she wasn't here.

Lily was still missing.

Thirteen

"I'll have to go back out," Matt said, as he unhooked a few of the dogs. His head throbbed with each pounding heartbeat.

Bandit shook and puffed out his chest. He pranced and panted happily, victorious. Matt spent a few precious seconds praising him.

"I'll keep my four regular dogs to go back over our trail," Matt told Tubbs.

"Should we tell your dad?" Tubbs asked.

Matt cringed at his question. If they told him, that would somehow make it real. Lily wasn't lost, she was just . . . missing. And Dad would be so angry. Maybe Matt could find her before his dad had to know.

"Let's try again first. She's got to be on the trail some-where."

"If she is, then how did we miss her?" Tubbs asked.

"Maybe she took a wrong turn," Matt said. Maybe she'd been lying in the snow, freezing to death, somewhere on a different trail all this time. Matt's hands shook with panic as he tried to change the gang line to a four-dog setup.

"We'll come help," Alex said. "Perhaps she's just hid-ing from you because she thinks you're mad at her. Maybe she'll come out for me?"

"Why would she do that?" Matt asked, angry.

"I'm a girl. I'm the youngest in my family. I can relate to her."

"You have an older brother?"

"Sister. Samantha is sixteen."

"Sam and Alex?" Tubbs asked. "Did your parents want boys or something?"

Alex heaved the bag of chicken that she'd taken out of the sled at him.

"Ready?" Matt called to the team.

Foo hesitated, glancing back at him. Leaving again so soon confused the dog.

"All right," Matt said. "Ahead, Foo. We've got to hurry."

Foo led the team out fast, sensing the urgency in Matt's voice.

"We'll try searching the trails we didn't go on," Matt said. "Maybe Lily didn't know where we turned. But after she fell off, Bandit knew where to find us by smelling our tracks."

As the dogs pulled them silently, they all peered into the trees along the trail. The only sound was the *shush* of the runners sliding across the snow and the tinkling of the dogs' neckline clips.

Into the tense quiet, Alex said, "When I was Lily's age, Sam was my hero. To me, she was like an idol that I looked up to. I wanted to be everywhere she was, do everything she was doing. She was always smarter than me. Better and faster, and I tried to keep up."

Guilt crept up Matt's throat. Lily just wanted to be with him. He had let her down. Why did he let everyone down?

And he couldn't imagine anyone smarter than Alex.

"Lily!" Matt called, over and over until he was hoarse.

They ran all the loops on the trail system, traveling only as far as Matt felt Lily might've gone and then turning around to head down another path.

Matt didn't realize how long their search was taking until he noticed the sun. It dipped low over the trees. Lily was still nowhere to be seen. And it was getting colder out. The wind pushed snow across the crusty surface of the trail, making hissing snow snakes.

Now Matt didn't care how much trouble he got into. He had to tell Dad. They had to find her.

"Let's go home," he said.

They climbed the last hill before the straight stretch, by the big pine where he could see the road to the mailboxes.

Alex suddenly called out, "Stop!"

Matt slammed the brake to stop the dogs, scanning for Lily. "What? Did you see something?" He sunk the snow hook.

Alex pointed up.

Tucked into the branches of the pine tree, Matt saw a blob of blue. He felt his chest explode.

"Lily!" he yelled, and raced toward the tree, leaving the team with Tubbs and Alex.

The blue blob stirred and Lily's head popped out. She stared down at Matt with bleary eyes.

"Lily! You . . . you fell asleep?" Matt was suddenly furious. "What the . . . ? Why are you . . . ? We were looking *everywhere* for you!"

Standing at the base of the tree, Matt held up his arms. He was going to murder her. Lily hopped down into them.

When Matt felt her body solid and real, he hugged her tightly. *She's okay.* His little sister was safe and not broken or bleeding or frozen. He must have held her a little too long, because she started to wriggle. Then he remembered he had an audience.

"Alex found you," Matt said. Then he paused to wonder about that. How had she known to look up into the trees, of all places?

"I knew she would," Lily said, running toward Alex.

"We went past here three times," Matt said. "Alex, I . . ." He didn't even know what to say.

"Think like a girl." Alex tapped her head. "When you're lost, go high. Nothing can get you up there. Also, you have a better view of your surroundings. It's simple logic."

Matt was so relieved to have found his sister that he didn't care how smart Alex was. Or how well she could run dogs. He was glad she was on his side.

"It's getting dark," Tubbs said.

Matt looked up and noticed that Tubbs was right. "Oh, no."

"My mom will be waiting." Tubbs heaved a sigh. "She'll be steamed."

"Mine too," Alex said, looking alarmed. "We should go."

They started back, none of them looking forward to the reception they would receive.

Fourteen

Just as they feared, their parents were waiting for them at the trailhead when they returned. Dad was hooking up a team, Matt assumed, to go find them. It made even Lily say, "Uh-oh."

"Yeah," Matt said.

Lily sat on Tubbs's lap in the sled. With only four sled dogs, Alex and Matt had been running beside the sled more than sharing the runners. By now, the dogs really needed those snacks.

"Matthew!" Dad yelled. He marched toward them with a mix of worry and fear and something else on his face. Matt was too nervous to try to figure it out.

"Where were you, son? Are you okay?"

"We're okay," Matt said, kicking in the hook and walking up the team to praise the dogs for their hard work.

Foo panted hotly in Matt's face and thumped his tail on the snow. Matt sank his fingers into the thick fur and pressed his forehead to the dog's. "Thank you," he whispered. "I promise . . . I . . ." He squeezed his eyes shut. Matt wanted to be worthy of Foo's trust.

"Why are you so late?" Dad asked. "Mrs. Stevens has been here for a long while." He nodded at Alex's mom and then eyed Matt sternly. Matt could imagine how much fun it'd been waiting here with her.

"And Mrs. White was about to call the searchers out for Tyler."

"Who?" Matt asked.

"That's me," said Tubbs with a sigh.

Tubbs's mom made a sweeping gesture toward their car. "Let's go, let's go. You've made me late for yoga!"

Alex's mom pointed a long finger at her daughter. "I don't believe this is the correct activity for you, Alexandria." She turned to Dad. "We will be withdrawing from the lessons, Mr. Misco. I'm sure you'll understand."

She turned to Matt next and gave him a withering

stare. Then he registered what she had said: Matt was losing a client.

No! He needed the sales. He needed to pass this assignment.

"Mrs. Stevens, he's never done this before, come back so late," Dad said. "Matt, what the dokee were you thinking, yeah?"

Matt couldn't think fast enough. He didn't want Dad to know how badly he'd screwed up with Lily. But his dad was angry already. And all the moms were mad at him.

"It was all my fault we're late!" Alex blurted. Tubbs and Matt both turned to stare at her.

"It had nothing to do with Matt. He was trying to be a good teacher. But I, well, I wanted to . . . run the team on my own! Yes, I took Lily here and made off with the team and left the boys to walk behind us. It was only a prank. Then I waited for them to catch up so we could all come in together." Her face was perfectly composed as she explained the situation to her mom.

"I'm going to be quite good at this, Mother. I just need to follow through with the rest of the planned lessons. I'm afraid I was showing off a little."

This, apparently, was just what Mrs. Stevens wanted to

hear. Her demeanor changed. The stiffness of her shoulders relaxed, her mouth turned up in a secret triumphant smile. She nodded a fraction before she stopped herself and smoothed down her long coat, picking off stray dog hairs.

"Well, we can discuss this at home. For now, we've been here long enough. If that's everything, Mr. Misco, we will call later in the week to let you know what we've decided."

Tubbs and Matt shared a look of amazement. First Alex had found Lily, and now she was covering for Matt. He had a new grudging respect for Alex, and he saw in Tubbs's eyes that he did too.

A horn blared and Tubbs jerked to a hasty shuffle. He retrieved Flute and then scampered toward his mom, who was waiting in the car.

Fifteen

"Whatcha seen, jellybeans?" Mom called when she came home that evening.

"A princess in her castle," Lily said, making Matt wonder if that was what she had been imagining in the tree.

The way Mom looked at him made him want to confess everything to her.

"A mad dad," Matt said.

Mom furrowed her brows and looked over at Dad.

He shook his head. "A sad dad."

"Bad dad," Lily piped in, not understanding the conversation.

"Is the dad sad about the lad?" Mom asked.

"More . . , glad," Dad said, crinkling his eyes.

At least Dad seemed to have forgiven Matt for being late and worrying everyone.

"Bad, mad, cad, dad," Lily chanted.

"Egad!" Mom said, and they both laughed loudly.

These were the kinds of conversations that made Matt wonder if he was adopted.

"I'm going to whittle," he said, heading to his room.

At least Lily hadn't tattled about their adventure. Matt had prepped her delicately, not wanting to make their version a big deal but trying to keep it a secret between them. It was bad enough he might lose a client and have to start all over with only two weekends left. But Matt had learned something today. And when Tubbs came over the next time, Matt would start doing things right.

In his room, Matt bent over his math book. What did he need for a balance sheet? Profits. How did he figure out profits, again? A pain started in his stomach.

Assets:
dogsleds
harnesses
gang line
sled dogs

<u>Expenses:</u>
coveralls $29
dog food $20 per month x dogs = ?

<u>Sales (2 clients):</u>
Tubbs $30
Alex $20
total $50

~~50 ÷ 29 =~~

~~29 ÷ 50 = $0.58~~

It was no use. Matt knew how to add and subtract well enough. He could multiply as long as he had the times table cheat sheet to check. But when it came to these problems, he didn't know what he was supposed to do. Which numbers should he divide by? Or were they supposed to be multiplied?

Matt ripped the sheet out of his workbook and scrunched it into a ball. He picked up his whittling knife. When he began to shape the little wooden dog's face, everything else seemed to fade.

"Matt?" Mom's voice was soft as she knocked on his door. It'd been a few years since she stopped tucking him in at night. He'd told her he was too old for it. But some nights he kind of missed it. Like tonight.

He sat up. "Yeah?"

She slipped in wearing a full-length nightgown with frilly collar, a polka-dot housecoat, and boot liners. Her normal eveningwear. She tiptoed toward the bed as if Matt were sleeping and then pounced on him, tickling him everywhere at once.

"Hey! Mom . . . stop!" he gasped. "Mom, come *on!*" He wriggled around, fending her off, trying not to laugh.

Mercifully she stopped and sat beside him to catch her breath. "How's your sled dog school coming along?"

"Good." He flicked one of the tassels on top of his quilt.

"So, tell me about it."

Matt shrugged. "Tubbs is cool, but he's hard to teach. Alex is a pain, but she's easy to teach."

Mom nodded sagely. "All teachers face challenges. Did you have a particularly hard day today?"

"Some days are harder than others."

Mom threw her head back to laugh. "Well said! That's a known fact."

She chuckled to herself before becoming serious. "Want to tell me what's got you so upset? Maybe I can help?"

Matt glanced at the crumpled paper in his trash bin. He considered just telling her everything—how hard math was, how much he wanted to pass, and how scared he was of being sent to the remedial class. How worried he was about disappointing her.

But he couldn't tell her any of that. She looked at him with that trusting expression, as if he were the smartest person in the world. She wanted him to work out how to fix his own troubles.

Use your mind, she'd said, after he'd gotten into that fight with Jacob.

"I'll figure it out," Matt said now.

"I never doubt that. You always deal with your challenges. I know how smart you are." She tapped his forehead and then brushed his hair off his face. Matt could smell the grapefruit lotion on her hand.

But her words didn't help. They just made him more anxious. He had to hide the fact that he didn't understand the formulas they were learning in math. Why didn't he, when everyone else did?

Matt tugged on the tassel savagely. How would he ace this project when he was supposed to have three clients to report on and now he might have only one?

Assignment Report #4

"There was a hockey game at the arena this weekend," Destin said as he taped a worksheet to the wall.

"Since my uncle's store is right beside the arena, my hot chocolate stand was way busy. Plus, we added cookies to the menu. We charged more than double the cost of making them because my mom said people would pay fifty cents for a homemade cookie. She was right. We sold out."

Hot Chocolate Stand by Destin Taylor

Cookie Expenses

cookie mix X 3 packages	$6.72
butter	$4.87
eggs	$1.84
total	$13.43

Cost of each cookie
$13.43 ÷ 72 cookies = $0.19 per cookie

Sales (lots of clients)
cookie price: $0.50 X 72 = $36
hot chocolate price: $0.50 X 100 = $50

Total time to bake and sell
5 hours

Salary
$50.57 net income ÷ 5 hours = $10.11 per hour

	Debit	Credit
income		$36.00
		$50.00
expenses	$13.43	
	$22.00	
total	$35.43	$86.00
net income		$50.57

"Ha-ha, sucker!" Jacob yelled. "Can I go next, Mr. Moffat? I made way more than that."

"That's perfect, Destin," Mr. Moffat said, ignoring Jacob. "Everyone, take a look at how Destin has made his calculations. Or you can also do this." He drew on the board:

(SALE PRICE - COST PER CUP) X NUMBER OF CUPS SOLD = PROFIT

"This is what I want to see for all businesses." Mr. Moffat clapped, then looked at Jacob and sighed. "Very well, Jacob, what do you have?"

Jacob ran to the front of the class as Destin rolled up his worksheet. "My customers told their friends and so this week I did nine houses," he said, proudly holding up a map of Wallace Street that showed his bottle collection route.

"With this business growth, my sales have grown."

As he held up a piece of cardboard with a chart drawn on it, Matt's heart sank. Everyone in the class so far had shown an increase in their business. Today he was supposed to show Mr. Moffat his numbers after getting three clients.

Matt rubbed his palms over the rough material of his jeans.

"Good job with the math, Jacob," Mr. Moffat said. "That's the way to do business. Happy customers make great advertising. But I'm amazed you were able to find so many willing to give their bottles away."

Mr. Moffat squinted at the map again, then shrugged. "Okay, whom haven't we heard from?"

Matt stayed absolutely still in his chair.

"Matthew! Almost missed you! How are your lessons?"

Matt walked slowly to the front as he tried to come up with what to say. When he turned to look at everyone, he hardly noticed the way they stared at him. He was too busy trying to think fast.

"My lessons are improving," he began. "We started using four dogs and now we've doubled that. One-hundred-percent increase in dogs."

"Well . . . I guess that sounds like some good growth." Mr. Moffat scratched his head, looking confused. "I'm not sure what that means, but I trust you do and that's what matters. I'm glad the operation of the business is a success. But do you have any numbers to show us?"

"Operating costs include things like coveralls that I had to provide for the client. They cost twenty-nine dollars. My assets include Foo and Grover and Fester and Tonka and Savage and Atlas and—"

"Yes, Matthew, thank you. Now you need to provide those numbers on *paper* so you can show us you know how to do the math."

Mr. Moffat stood and, to Matt's relief, addressed the rest of the class. "I want to see net sales, profit and loss statements, and how much you're making per hour, just like we've been learning since September. One more report before the assignment is due, people!"

Matt nodded and smiled to show how confident he felt. It was becoming easier to stand up here. He could even look at Rhonda and Jeff in the front row, and Mr. Moffat could hear him now. No more mumbling.

When he sat back down, he let out a breath. He had another week to find more clients. And to figure out the numbers.

Sixteen

"**W**e're finally doing it," Matt told Tubbs when he arrived at the Miscos' house on Friday after school.

Tubbs eyed him nervously.

"You're going to run Flute," Matt announced. "And do it on your own."

"I'm not sure I'm ready for that."

"Well, not today. But you both will be by the end of our lessons. I promised, didn't I?"

"But I still haven't found you a third client," Tubbs pointed out. "And . . . is Alex coming back?"

"I don't know."

They both paused and looked sad.

"Well . . . can you use your mom and dad as clients?"

"Mr. Moffat says no family members. That way it's a real business." Matt watched Tubbs sit on an upside-down bucket next to the barn door. Everything about him was big. His eyes were permanently round, as if trying to take in all the amazing things in life at once. His curiosity about the world was as big as a house, and his smile was even bigger. He had tried to help Matt get clients. It was time Matt helped him.

"Let's focus on Flute now."

At that news, Tubbs straightened and leaned forward.

"Here's the plan," Matt said. "We're going to run a three-dog team with Flute beside Bandit."

"Oh. I thought you were going to teach him obedience. To sit and stay and stuff like that," Tubbs said. He quickly added, "But this sounds okay too."

"We're starting with this. Flute knows Bandit, so he can learn from him. Then if that works, tomorrow you can run those two dogs to chase my team. Two dogs are easier to run than four. Plus you don't have to share the runners if you're on your own. You'll be better balanced. And with those two young dogs, you'll go fast. The faster you go, the easier it is to steer."

"That doesn't sound right."

"I know I haven't been the best teacher. But just . . . trust me."

So far this had been Matt's Sled Dog School of Having Really Bad Experiences and Then Just Trying Not to Repeat Them. He finally understood Dad's favorite saying: *Good judgment comes from experience, and experience comes from poor judgment.*

It was time for good judgment.

Matt wanted his school to show people how amazing the dogs were. And he wanted Tubbs to have fun outside, to not be afraid.

"This will be the mushing test," Matt said. "Hook up and run two dogs on your own. Watch them smile and keep them safe, and you'll pass the lessons."

After Matt prepared Foo in lead and gave Tubbs a harness that would fit Flute, they went to get Tubbs's dog from the pen. Flute stuck his head through the padding of the harness with no problem. But when Tubbs tried to pull Flute's legs through the webbing, the dog leaped up and bonked him in the chin. Flute tangled, tripped, and fell headfirst into the snow, pulling Tubbs with him.

Matt took the harness from Tubbs. "Easier to hold him between your knees."

When Flute wasn't looking, Matt stood over the dog, held him firmly with his legs, and stuffed the harness over his head. This time when the dog jumped, Matt was ready for it. He slid the harness under the Lab's feet and pulled the tug line across the dog's back in one smooth motion.

"You make it look so easy," Tubbs said.

When Flute felt the tug of the harness, he looked down at his chest, then back at Matt. He lowered his head and pulled Matt toward the sled, his tail wagging furiously.

"I think he wants to do this!" Tubbs shouted.

Matt brought Bandit to stand beside Flute and held his breath. But Bandit immediately recognized his buddy. They touched noses while Matt quickly hooked in the yearling.

As soon as Tubbs and Matt left them to run back to the sled, the dogs jumped each other, Flute's front feet snagging inside Bandit's harness. Foo stood in single lead, impatiently watching them over his shoulder. Matt pulled them apart and hauled Flute over the gang line and back onto his side.

Foo stared down the trail and barked with excitement. The rest of the dogs in the yard voiced their frustration in high-pitched shrieks. Matt felt just as anxious to go as the screaming dogs. Their eagerness was contagious.

"You're going to have to hold them before we take off running," Matt said to Tubbs. "I'll grab you on the way by."

Tubbs stared at him, dubious. "You're gonna do what, now?"

"Don't worry. It's a thing. Done it lots of times," Matt called over his shoulder as he raced to the sled. "Just keep the dogs from tying themselves into knots for a second." He pulled the snub line that attached them to the tree and popped the snow hook.

"Get ready!" Matt yelled.

Tubbs moved over as the dogs whipped past him. When Matt got close, Tubbs stretched out his arms with a look of absolute terror on his face. They both reached for each other at the same time. Tubbs clung to the handlebar and jumped onto a runner. He bent over the bar to find his balance, nearly falling, but Matt held him.

When Tubbs straightened, his face shone. "I did it!"

They both laughed, the cold wind hitting Matt's teeth. He felt as if he'd just gotten an A on a report card—which was weird. He jumped onto the runners all the time. It was no big deal.

But suddenly it was.

He was proud of Tubbs. Helping him made Matt feel better than he had in a long time.

Matt punched him in the arm. "You did it!"

"I. Am. A musher!" Tubbs yelled, and tried to dance, but Matt had to grab him to remind him he was sliding along a trail, balancing on a runner. They clung to the handlebar next to each other in silence for a while. It was as if they didn't have to say anything to know what the other meant. Matt had never had a friend like this.

Matt watched Flute, who was the whole point to this quest, really. That crazy dog didn't seem to have any trouble fitting in. He charged down the trail, his long legs galloping awkwardly. The best mix in any dog team was to have experienced dogs for wisdom and young dogs for passion. Bandit was like the spark plug of the team. And now, so was Flute.

Flute looked over his shoulder at the boys a few times. "You're fine, Flute. Good dog! You're doing great!"

Flute faced forward again and pulled with all his heart. The dog had *heart*.

And Bandit pulled beside him with unrestrained joy. They weren't matching their strides yet or anything, but they were both pulling like mad. The team skimmed along the trail, the trees whipped past, and Matt's smile was freezing on his face.

✿ ✿ ✿

That night Matt sanded the sled dog he'd whittled while he tried to find in his math book how to get the cost per unit. He heard the phone ring. Dad talked with someone for a while before stomping toward Matt's room. Matt closed his book. As usual, his dad swung the door wide, nearly falling into the room.

"That was Mrs. Stevens, Alexandria's mom."

Matt tensed. "Is she letting Alex back?"

"Seems so. But she's coming back on a condition."

"What condition?"

"Well, it's very strange. She's an . . . unusual woman."

If Dad was calling her unusual and strange, Matt couldn't even imagine what this condition was.

"What? What does she want?"

"Prepare yourself, son. Things are about to get weird around here."

Seventeen

$\mathbb{D}$ad was right. It was weird.

Saturday morning Tubbs and Matt were about to cross the bridge to the barn when they heard Alex's car arrive. It was followed by two more cars and a van. A whole bunch of people Matt didn't know gathered in the driveway while Alex's mom ordered everyone where to stand.

"Go get the huskies, Alexandria. Make sure they're the pretty huskies."

"Sorry 'bout this," Alex mumbled to Matt and Tubbs. Lily joined them in the driveway.

"What's going on?" Tubbs asked.

"Mom works for channel nine," Alex said, jerking her thumb behind her at the cameramen piling out of the news van. "She's a reporter for the local community news, and she wants this to be one of her lead stories this week."

"As in, we're going to be on TV?" Tubbs asked, eyes wide. "Holy smoley! Wait till I tell my grandma!"

"More like, I'm going to be on TV. Me and my mom," Alex said, staring at her boots.

Tubbs did an awkward dance of excitement, hopping up and down, his red cheeks quivering. "And I know you! I'm going to know someone on TV!"

Tubbs seemed to be incapable of a bad thought even if it hit him over the head. But Matt didn't have that trouble. He narrowed his eyes at the scene in his driveway.

When Alex turned to him, they both stared at each other. Lily was silent for once, waiting. But Matt couldn't be angry at Alex for this. Despite what a pain she was, he was happy he hadn't lost a client. If he let himself think about it, Alex wasn't just a client anymore. Matt was actually happy she was there. He was glad they hadn't lost *her*.

Then he noticed that Alex and her mom were wearing matching outfits. He *really* couldn't be mad at her now. Poor Alex. Her cheeks flamed red.

"Well, at least Lily has another girl around here again," Matt said.

Alex's shoulders relaxed. "Matt, they want to get a shot of me running the team on the trail. Who do you think I should use?"

Then they were all busily hooking up dogs and planning the shot with the cameramen while Alex's mom barked orders as if she were a director. Dad looked on with an incredulous expression on his face. Lily trailed Alex around until Mrs. Stevens gently but firmly moved her out of the shot.

Matt, of course, chose Grover and Foo in lead because they were dependable. He picked Atlas for wheel, hardly noticing the dog's stubby tail, his coarse fur, and the rip in his ear from a dogfight when he was in his prime. And beside him Matt used Savage because Alex's mom wanted "pretty."

Tubbs, Alex, and Matt ran the dogs down the trail a short distance before turning the team around. And then the boys helped prepare Alex for her film debut.

Tubbs fixed her hat, smoothing her hair away from her face.

Matt stood on the snow hook while giving last-minute advice. "Just feather the brake like I showed you. And don't forget to set the hook before you leave the sled."

"Got it," Alex said.

"Rolling in three, two, one . . ." a cameraman called to them.

Alex reached for the hook and Matt stepped away, letting her take the team. The dogs charged toward the cameraman, eyes blazing, tongues out, smiling like professionals. Alex stood perfectly balanced on the runners.

And that's when Matt caught a flash of fur out of the corner of his eye.

How did the puppies get out? No matter—they were here now, with Dragon leading the escape. Matt partially covered his eyes as he realized where the puppies were heading.

Straight for Alex's team.

They bounded over the snow with fierce focus. At eight weeks, they were about the size of determined bowling balls.

Matt started running. "Slow down!" he yelled at Alex.

But he was too far behind and the puppies were too fast. They darted straight at Grover, their favorite dog. In the yard, he was easy-natured, one of the only dogs to allow the pups to climb over him and hang off his ears and lips.

As the pups reached the team, they barreled into Grover. He tripped, pulling Foo down with him. The wheel dogs crashed on top of them, creating a mad pileup of dogs and teeth and puppy screams.

The sled stopped dead.

Alex was pitched into the air and sailed in an impressive arc over all the chaos. Then she tumbled and landed at the feet of the cameraman.

"Alexandria!" Mrs. Stevens screamed.

"Grover!" Dad yelled.

"Got it!" the cameraman shouted.

By the time Matt reached them, Alex was up and Dad had the team untangled. The dogs were all jazzed. Wide-mouthed grins, shining eyes. That had been *fun*.

"Lily, get these pups to the pen," Dad said.

"What kind of sled school is this?" Mrs. Stevens demanded.

Alex had her back to Matt, her shoulders shaking as if she was sobbing. Matt felt a stab of fear for her. "Alex! Are you okay?"

She turned to him, her face streaked in tears.

From *laughing*.

"That was so awesome!" she said. "Did you see the look on my mother's face?"

The TV crew, along with Dad and Mrs. Stevens, argued among themselves while Matt, Alex, and Tubbs helped Lily round up the puppies, who raced in circles around Mrs. Stevens. How did they know who would give them the biggest reaction?

Mrs. Stevens kept yelling something about editing the film or "heads would roll." Dad managed to convince her to let Alex stay while Mrs. Stevens sorted everything out with the TV crew *back at the station*.

It was all as weird as Dad said it would be. Mrs. Stevens was the strangest of them all. Matt was starting to see that maybe his parents weren't the bad kind of weird.

After the circus left, it was just Matt, Alex, and Tubbs. Matt needed to remember to thank Dad later, for sending Alex's mom away.

"Well, that was interesting," he said.

"I liked the part when Alex flew through the air," Tubbs said.

Alex just grinned at them.

After all the craziness that had just happened, Matt knew he needed to deliver a coach speech to inspire everyone. The best he could do was quote the plaque that Mom had hung above the couch: SUCCESS AGAINST HARDSHIP AND CHALLENGE BUILDS CONFIDENCE AND SELF-ESTEEM.

There was a long pause.

Tubbs shuffled his feet.

Matt tried again. "Now, do you guys want to learn something or what?"

Alex and Tubbs raised their fists and cheered.

They hooked up three teams of two dogs each. This time, Matt taught everything the right way. He explained how to hit the brake before a turn and then steer into it. He showed them how to pull on the handlebar and bend the sled to cut a corner. And he showed them how to brace themselves on the runners, to absorb the ruts in the trail through their legs.

But the best part was when Matt talked about the dogs. He demonstrated how to hold a dog between his knees in order to gain enough control to harness the wiggling animal. How to watch their ears and their tails when they ran for signs of trouble.

"Dogs talk to us through their bodies," Matt said. "We have to listen to how they're feeling when they're on the gang line. Always, always, watch the dogs. It's the most important thing."

Matt noticed how he could read the faces of his students, too. They shone with understanding. His friends got it. Lily had joined them for the last part of the lesson, and her face was shining too.

They ran the teams one after the other. First Matt

lined up with Grover and Foo, with Lily in his sled. Then Tubbs set up with Flute and Bandit, followed by Alex running Savage and Atlas. They pulled their snub lines one by one and took off.

Tubbs hung on, his glee big enough to melt the North Pole.

"I'm doing it! Matt!" he yelled. "Do you see me?"

"Yes, I can see you, Tubbs. I'm right here!" Matt laughed over his shoulder.

"Does Alex see me? I can't turn around."

"I see you, Tubbs!" Alex screamed from behind them. "You're doing great!"

"Look at Flute!" Tubbs continued yelling at Matt. He could hardly contain himself.

Lily laughed in Matt's sled. He watched his dogs and felt himself glowing.

"You should keep your school forever!" Lily said.

Matt's good feelings evaporated. He remembered he had to do his fifth assignment report tomorrow, and then he had to hand in his final project report the following week. He did not have three clients. He was going to fail the class.

Assignment Report #5

"This is the last report before assignments are due," Mr. Moffat said, as if it were the best news in the world. "I'm eager to hear what you all have for me today. Let's start with Tammy."

Normally Tammy marched when she walked anywhere. A particular way of strutting that Matt could recognize from across a field. So he was surprised to see Tammy slink past him on her way to the front of the class. When she turned around, everyone gasped.

Her lips were bright red and puffy. Huge. The rest of her face was blotchy and sort of swollen. Tears spilled out of her red-rimmed eyes.

"My little brother put cayenne pepper into the Cinnabon-bon pot. He swapped it for the cinnamon. They look the same!" she wailed. "It ruined the whole batch. We had customers returning their Cinnabon-bon, plus the unopened jars of different flavors they'd bought in case those were ruined too. They told us they'd warn people away from our lip-gloss. I didn't understand until I tested the Cinnabon-bon on myself this morning."

"Oh, dear," Mr. Moffat said above everyone's laughter. "I trust no one was seriously hurt. But did you do the math for your business?"

"Oh, yes, my mom made me add up all the expenses. She said she'd told me not to buy so many ingredients, but I wanted to have a good variety." Tammy inserted her flash drive into the laptop. "My business would've been great if my brother hadn't wrecked it. My whole project is a failure!"

Homemade Lip-Gloss by Tammy Fuller

Expenses

white beeswax pellets	$11
shea butter	$7
vitamin E oil	$6
extra ingredients	$9
flavoring oils @ $5 X 6 =	$30
mini lip-gloss jars (50)	$28
total:	$91

Cost of each jar of lip-gloss

$91 ÷ 50 jars = $1.82 per jar

Sales (many clients)

11	Cherrylicious
1	Banana Manga

2   Blueberry Blaster
8   Choco Smoothie
6   Strawberry Sparkle
8   Gorgeous Grapefruit
9   Cinnabon-bon
45   total = 45 jars sold

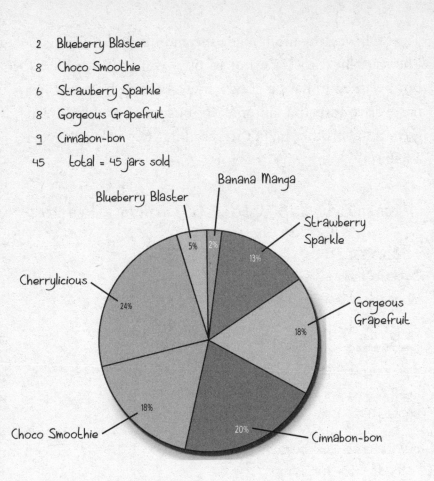

total sales: 45 jars sold x $3.60 per jar = $162.00
loss of sales: 22 jars returned x $3.60 per jar = $79.20

<u>Total time to make and sell</u>
5 hours per week x 5 weeks = 25 hours

	DEBIT	CREDIT
income		$162.00
expenses	$91.00	
total	$91.00	$162.00
minus returns	$79.20	
		net income -$8.20

Tammy's laser pointer quivered over the last line. "I don't even know how to calculate how much my salary was per hour when my business lost money!"

"Tammy, this is fantastic!" Mr. Moffat clapped his hands. "The assignment wasn't about making a *successful* business, it was to show the numbers. You've done this brilliantly! Some businesses operate at a loss for the first year. This teaches us a lesson in expenses, doesn't it? All entrepreneurs need to balance the needs of the business with their budget! I love your math. Great work. Looks like your report is ready to hand in."

Tammy blinked. "R-really? It is?" She wiped her nose. "I did predict Cherrylicious would be a top seller." She stood straighter, retrieved her flash drive, and marched back to her seat.

Mr. Moffat scanned his sheet. "Jacob, how's business?"

Jacob didn't move from his seat.

"Jacob? Do you have a report?"

"Nope."

"We all have to report. What happened?"

"Had to return the money," Jacob mumbled.

"What's that? You have a loss too? That's okay, as I've said. Just need to see the numbers in your assignment when you hand it in next week. Why did you return the money?"

"Um . . . I might have mentioned the bottle drive was for charity."

"What?" Mr. Moffat yelled.

Everyone in the room sat straighter and shut up. Mr. Moffat never yelled.

Jacob shuffled to the front of the room through the deathly quiet. "My clients *assumed* it was for a charity. I just told them it was for school. That's what they wanted to hear. But then Mr. Lewis asked my dad about it at the Beef and Burp, and Dad sort of lost it."

"I'll need to speak with you later, Jacob. And your parents. Sit down, please." Mr. Moffat stalked back to his desk and wrote a note. He took his glasses off and cleaned them with his tie.

"Mr. Misco. How is everything with you? Are you working on your final sales report?"

Matt stood. "Well . . . we had a full house this weekend. Couldn't fit one more car in our driveway."

"Wow! That's impressive. I can't tell you how pleased I am to hear that. I'm so proud of you, and I can't wait to read your final report. Okay, let's open our workbooks."

Jacob's problem seemed to have distracted Mr. Moffat from noticing that Matt didn't have any numbers either. He wondered how impressed and proud his teacher would be next week when he learned that Matt didn't have the required three clients.

Eighteen

Friday night, Tubbs called Matt seconds before Mrs. Stevens's news report was aired on the local television station.

"Okay, it's on," he said breathlessly, then squealed with delight. "There's Flute!"

Tubbs described the clip in detail as he watched. "Alex and her mom are standing around. Now Alex and her mom are talking about dogsledding. They just said, 'Matt's Sled Dog School,' but I don't see you," Tubbs reported.

"Mrs. Stevens is saying how great her daughter is at everything she does," Tubbs said. "And how dogsledding is another unique sport that her daughter has . . . incorporated into her productive schedule of . . . um . . . I can't understand what she's saying, really. But she keeps petting her fur coat like it's going to start barking. I think she likes talking about Alex."

"Poor Alex," Matt said. He wished he could see the TV report for himself.

"Wait. Now they're showing the part with the crash. Oh . . . there she goes! You can even see Alex's grin as she's flying through the air. Yeah, sounds like Mrs. Stevens screaming in the background. Now, that's entertaining TV!"

As soon as Matt got off the phone with Tubbs, the phone rang again.

"Is this Matt's Sled Dog School?" an all-too-familiar voice asked. "We just saw it on TV and I want to sign up."

Dread flowed through Matt's veins. This was what he wanted. He'd have three clients. Just in time, he'd be able to hand in his final assignment next week. But the voice on the other line made his heart hammer. Yet he had no choice.

"Yup," Matt said. "I don't know why you're all of a sudden interested in my project, Jacob. But you can start tomorrow. It's ten bucks a week, cash only. We meet in my yard at ten in the morning. You know where to find it."

❉ ❉ ❉

Jacob's car pulled into the driveway Saturday morning. Matt kept thinking it had just been some joke he was trying to pull. But there Jacob was, stepping out of his mom's Jeep and looking around imperiously.

"'Sup, Smokey?"

"Stop calling me that." Matt had just finished cleaning the dog yard and really wished he wasn't holding a poop shovel.

"Okay, don't get your panties in a twist. I'm just playing with you."

Cool as he could, Matt hurried to the barn and leaned the shovel against the side where it belonged. As Jacob's mom drove away, the dogs started up a happy howl. They had warm chicken broth in their bellies and a clean yard, and they knew they were going for a run soon. Life was good enough to sing about.

Matt glanced over to see Foo on top of his doghouse with his head thrown back, his ruffed neck stretched out. His long, low howl wavered and curled around the others'. Matt could pick out each distinct voice. Savage had the nicest howl, rich and wonderful. And then the pups started up from their pen. They were getting louder, not better, but they tried.

"Hey, listen to the dogs! They're celebrating that I'm here. When do we get started, yo?"

Somehow, Jacob's voice ruined the whole song.

"We have to wait for the others to get here before we start. I have a lesson plan."

"That girl from TV?"

"Yeah, and my friend Tubbs." Matt didn't know why he felt the need to stress that Tubbs was his friend. He stared at Jacob and remembered the last time he'd been here. Matt couldn't believe he'd ever thought Jacob was his friend. And now Jacob was back at his house.

At least Dad was watching Lily today. He'd finally finished his big pottery order, and things were going back to normal. Matt glanced at Jacob again. *Normal for us, anyway,* Matt thought.

As soon as Tubbs's minivan showed up, Matt let out a relieved sigh. He was like a dog with his pack at his back. He felt bigger, as though he could face down an intruder, as long as he wasn't alone.

But when Jacob watched Tubbs climb out of his vehicle with Flute and huff over to them, Jacob's eyes widened and a smirk crept over his face. A hot feeling flooded through Matt.

Alex arrived right after Tubbs. For a long moment, they all just stood there eyeing one another. Both Alex and Jacob were busy looking down their noses at each other, which would have been funny to Matt any other time.

Matt was just realizing he should probably say something when Flute made an unexpected dash for the dog yard. Tubbs tripped over the snow, fell onto his face, and let go of the leash. Matt met Tubbs's eyes, full of worry, before they all ran after the Lab.

Flute beelined straight to Atlas, his leash trailing behind. Were they going to have a dogfight before Jacob even started the lesson?

Flute skidded to a halt right before he reached the old dog. Amazingly, he dropped his head at the last moment and approached with a submissive crawl. Atlas sniffed him and then promptly ignored him. Tubbs and Matt gaped at each other and then started laughing.

"The dogs love him now!" Tubbs said.

"Yeah, I think Bandit told them that Flute's all right," Matt said, "even though he's not like them."

"That is fascinating," Alex said, gesturing excitedly toward the dogs. "Watch them! Atlas is telling all the other dogs now. He's communicating the way the *Canis lupus* does, with his whole demeanor."

When she noticed the expressions on Tubbs's and Matt's faces, she shrugged and then grinned. "I studied *Canis lupus* behavior for a school project once. That's gray wolf. Even though dogs are a subspecies of wolves, *Canis lupus familiaris*, they speak the same language."

As they watched, Atlas approached Flute. Flute rolled onto his back. Matt was shocked to see Atlas do a play bow, inviting Flute to join. Flute leaped up and began racing in circles.

"Yeah!" Tubbs did a little jig of excitement.

Jacob started laughing, but he wasn't laughing with them. He was laughing *at* Tubbs.

Matt's whole body stiffened. He suddenly recalled all the times Jacob had made fun of his family—how he had everyone chanting "Smokey" on the bus, how he had told everyone Matt's family drank curdled milk—and all of it came together inside Matt and exploded out.

He turned on Jacob. "Don't laugh at him. Why are you so rotten? I'm not letting you make fun of anyone here. Especially not my friends."

Jacob stopped laughing and turned to face Matt with a

puzzled expression. "You have friends? That's funny. Only you would have a Goodyear blimp and a teacher's-pet wolf-girl as friends. A whale and a wolf-girl." He laughed too loudly at his own joke.

Matt stood in front of Tubbs. Wordlessly, Alex joined him. With the tense silence in the wake of Jacob's words, even the dogs had gone quiet. Watching. Matt's hands curled into fists at his sides.

Suddenly, he remembered Mom's words about dealing with things by using his mind, not his fists. He glanced at Tubbs. His friend was looking at the ground. He was acting as if he was used to bullies like Jacob. Did he get teased at school too?

Matt only knew he didn't want Jacob anywhere near Tubbs.

"Why are you even here?" Matt asked Jacob.

"I saw how fast the dogs ran on TV," Jacob said. "I want to have them pull me like that."

"Dogs can sense a good person, you know," Matt said. "They can tell if someone's rotten. They know what you're like inside just from your smell. Did you know that? Do you think we should bring you over to Atlas there and get him to smell you? He nearly ripped someone's face off last week because they didn't say please and thank you. What do you think he'll do to you?"

Jacob looked at Atlas uneasily. "That's dumb. As if."

"Yeah," Tubbs said. "Last week was bad. There was blood everywhere. Atlas is a killer."

Alex and Matt stared at Tubbs. He stared at Jacob.

"That dog doesn't look so tough," Jacob finally said. "He's not fighting with Fatso's dog, and that dog looks about as dumb as a stump."

"That's it. You're not getting lessons."

"What? You can't do that." Jacob's expression shifted slightly—he almost looked desperate. His shoulders sagged as though they were suddenly tired of bearing a weight.

"I need to . . . I have to hide out for the day," he said with a small voice. "Dad's on a rampage about the whole bottle drive thing. I have to stay out of his way."

Matt felt uneasy that Jacob seemed to have finally said something true. But Matt still needed to protect his friends. "This is my school. I make the rules."

Jacob's expression turned steely again. "But I'm a paying customer. And don't you *need* all your paying customers?"

Jacob was right. Matt did need them.

"The dogs only pull real mushers. You have to take the lessons to become a musher, and you can't, because . . ." Matt took a deep breath. "Because I'm not teaching you. You're expelled."

Nineteen

As they all watched Jacob leave, Matt watched his last chance to pass the school project leave too. With the final report due Monday morning, there was no time left to have enough sales to show what Mr. Moffat was asking for. Matt needed three clients, and he had only two. Even he could do that math.

"Well, now that *he's* gone, we can have some fun," Alex said. "Nice one about the face-ripping-off part."

Matt shrugged. "I was improvising."

"The dogs don't really do that, right?" Tubbs said.

"Not the face thing, but they do smell people."

"Wish they had been around during summer camp when I left a candy bar in my sleeping bag," Tubbs said.

"Would've been easier than trying to explain to everyone that it was *chocolate* all over my pajamas."

"Augh!" Alex covered her face. "TMI, Tubbs!"

"No one would smell my PJs to believe me!" Tubbs continued.

"Let's get the sleds ready, Hershey," Matt said, giving Tubbs a knock on the shoulder.

When they laid out the gang line, Matt noticed one of the tugs was almost chewed through.

"Yikes, I have to fix this first," he said, separating the tug line from the gang line. Finding new lines in the barn, Matt started measuring and cutting.

"How do you know how long these should be?" Tubbs asked, watching Matt splice the ends into loops with a wooden fid.

"I just measure the length minus the loop at the end," Matt said. "Look—the tug lines should all be equal lengths, long enough for the dogs to reach the neckline, but not too long, or they'll get tangled."

Matt stretched out the lines and noticed with satisfaction they were all the same. Then he raced to the house to ask Lily if she wanted to come, even though Dad was watching her.

They ran three teams of two all the way to the base camp. No one fell off, lost their team, or got dragged.

When they returned to the barn, they watched as the dogs lay in the snow, still harnessed, and gnawed on their snacks of fist-size frozen chicken. Grover growled and eyed Foo suspiciously. The dogs turned so they were facing away from each other, but their backs still touched. Snowflakes fell lightly onto the dogs' fur.

"Flute is like one of the team now," Tubbs said, sitting on his overturned bucket. "Thanks to Bandit."

Lily, sitting on Alex's lap, lighted up as if she were the one who'd been praised.

"Lily," Matt said, "why do you always pick Bandit when you want to run the dogs? What is it about him out of all the dogs in the yard?"

"I love him. He's my favorite."

"But why?"

She shrugged and stopped braiding Alex's hair long enough to look at Matt. "He's the youngest, besides the new puppies. And no one thinks he's ready to run. But he told me he is! Sometimes I come out when no one else is around, and he tells me things."

Matt immediately recalled his own nights with Foo,

sleeping in the pen with him. Sometimes, you just had a soul connection with a dog and you couldn't explain it to anyone.

He nodded at his sister. "Maybe he'll be your lead dog one day, Lil."

She looked at Matt as if to say, *Well, duh!* and went back to Alex's hair.

For a moment, there was no sound but the dogs' lips smacking as they chewed with their mouths open.

A sadness hit Matt. This was their last class together. He'd just gotten the hang of being a teacher. He'd miss the teaching, but most of all, he would miss running with Tubbs and Alex.

Matt picked up the bag he had hidden in the corner of the barn in preparation for this moment. He peeked inside with satisfaction. Yes, this was the right decision. Last night, when he remembered he had promised musher certificates, he knew what would be the perfect prize.

"Everyone passed the test to complete Matt's Sled Dog School," he announced, reaching into the bag. "Everyone made it to the base camp and back with their own team."

Matt pulled out the whittled sled dog he'd finished last night with a final polish of sandpaper. The final piece to his whittled six-dog team. But instead of placing it in the glass display case in his room, he had carefully printed with a fine-tipped marker the words JUNIOR MUSHER. And on the other side he'd written SLED DOG SCHOOL GRADUATE. He'd taken the other lead dog from the display and written the same on that one, too.

He presented them to Tubbs and Alex.

"Did you make this?" Alex asked with surprise. "Wow! This is good!"

Tubbs's eyes widened as he accepted his sled dog and ran his fingers over the dog's pointed ears. "Thanks for the cat!"

Matt's face fell.

"Joking!" Tubbs said, nudging him. "This is amazing! Junior musher!" He hooted with delight. Watching him dance, Matt smiled. He might've failed the project, but at least he hadn't failed his friends.

❊ ❊ ❊

Monday morning Matt woke up early and considered playing sick. He lay in bed for a while before he remembered that sick people in his house didn't get to play with the dogs, and they didn't get a story. They were forced to eat chicken soup, which Matt hated. And it was really boring to stay home all day.

Besides, he had to face the fact that he'd failed to complete the project. Today or tomorrow would yield the same result. So he got up and wrote down what he knew. But his numbers included only two clients. And he still hadn't worked out how much they spent on dog food for six weeks. He had the total for a month, though, and he figured that was enough. He would count five dogs that he had to feed—the five plus Flute that he, Alex, and Tubbs had used in their final run on Saturday, before graduating. But he didn't know what to do with the rest of the numbers.

MATT'S SLED DOG SCHOOL BY MATT MISCO

Assets
dogsleds
harnesses
gang line
sled dogs

Expenses:
coveralls $29
dog food $20 per month per dog
used 5 dogs: ~~20 + 5 = $25~~
$20 x 5 = $100

<u>Sales (2 clients)</u>
Tubbs $50
Alex $40 (4 weeks)
total: $90

He shut his book in disgust and jammed it into his backpack. Thinking about everyone finding out he had to take the remedial math class almost made him sick for real.

❊ ❊ ❊

After chores, Matt was putting on his school coat when the dogs started up a ruckus. He peered out the window to see Tubbs's minivan pulling into the driveway. Confused, Matt ran outside to meet him. Why was Tubbs here before school? Matt's bus would show up any minute.

Tubbs spied him as he climbed out the side door of the van. He started to wave, missed a step, and fell out onto the snow. But he bounced up, a huge grin splitting his face.

"What's going on?" Matt asked.

"Guess what? You'll never guess. Holy smoley, I should make you guess. Can you guess? Or do you need a clue? I should give you a—"

"*Tubbs!* Come on, I'm going to miss my bus. What is it?"

As Tubbs waved an envelope in front of Matt, Tubbs's dad yelled out the van door. "Let's go! I said one minute!"

Tubbs thrust the envelope into Matt's hands, grinned, then dived back into the vehicle. As he slid the door shut, he yelled, "I'm like a drive-by delivery hero. So cool! Call you tonight."

The bus arrived as the minivan skidded out of the driveway. Matt shoved the envelope into his pocket and raced inside. He grabbed his backpack, yelling goodbye, and then sprinted for the bus. Lily's little bus was already coming down the road by the time he reached his.

Mrs. Wilson scowled at him and then shut the door with a dramatic crank of the large lever. Matt slid into the first empty seat and took out the envelope. He stared at the crisp handwriting.

MATTHEW MISCO

When he tore open the envelope, the first thing he noticed was all the money. More bills than he was used to holding. He snatched the letter that was attached and started to read.

Matthew—

Enclosed is payment for Tyler for five weeks of dogsledding lessons. Also included is payment for Flute. You have done something marvelous with this dog. He has been well-behaved in the house since you started training him. I thank you for doing a good job. I will tell my friends about your dog training services.

—Mrs. White

The letter dropped into Matt's lap. He sifted through the cash. One hundred dollars? He glanced around as if looking for a hidden camera, because this was so weird.

Training? He hadn't trained Flute. Not obedience training the way Tubbs had expected. Matt had just gotten the dog running. Come to think of it, Flute had had so much fun running with the team, he put all of his energy into it.

Matt didn't think the Lab had been used to the

exercise. All dogs needed exercise. Flute had probably been crazy in the house all the time because he hadn't had any way to let out his energy. Running in the team kept him happy, and he must've been quieter in the house afterward.

Matt had to read the letter again before he realized what this meant. It was as if the sun found all the windows in the bus at once and shone in, covering everything with light. Matt's whole body hummed with relief.

Flute is my third client.

Twenty

All the way to school Matt studied examples in his math book. He still couldn't figure out which numbers to multiply and which to divide.

It was like staring at a locked door without the key. His mind didn't work in neat rows. It was more messy.

As the bus pulled in front of the school, Matt wrote down the three sales for the project, still amazed at the fact that he had gotten all three clients. He carefully added the numbers. At least he knew that much. After he wrote out the rest, he tried to figure out what he was supposed to do next.

MATT'S SLED DOG SCHOOL BY MATT MISCO

Assets
dogsleds
harnesses
gang line
sled dogs

Expenses:
coveralls	$29
dog food ($20 x 5 dogs =)	$100
total:	$129

Sales (3 clients)
Tubbs	$50
Alex	$40 (4 weeks)
Flute	$50
total:	$140

	Debit	Credit
income		$140
expenses	$129	
total		
net income:		

140 ÷ 129=

Total time to teach lessons
24 hours: 3 hours for every Saturday (5),
Sunday (1), Wednesday (1), and Friday (1)

Salary:

Matt was so absorbed by the calculations, he didn't even hear Jacob approach until the page was torn from his hands.

"What? Didn't finish your assignment?" Jacob smirked. "Guess you shouldn't have kicked out your last client, huh?"

Matt held out his hand for the sheet. "I didn't need you, Jacob. I had others. Real mushers. Give it."

Jacob peeked at the figures. "Handwritten? This looks like trash." He pulled out his own final report. "I did mine on the computer like a professional."

Matt had time only to see Jacob's neat columns and rows before Jacob snapped the book shut. He tossed Matt's page over his shoulder. "Good luck with that, loser."

Mrs. Wilson watched Jacob leave. Matt suddenly realized he was the last one on the bus. He picked up the page and stuffed it into his backpack as he hurried down the aisle. He expected the driver to grumble at him for making her wait.

"Let me see what you have there," she said instead.

Matt showed her, too embarrassed to know what else to do.

As Mrs. Wilson looked over the numbers, she took out a pencil from the visor above her. "Don't pay him any mind," she said gruffly. "He's just jealous of you."

"Jealous? Why would he be jealous of me?"

She checked behind Matt before leaning closer. "You have loving, supportive parents, don't you?" She lowered her voice. "Try to be kind. I know it's difficult when others take out their troubles on us."

She studied Matt's page. "You should remember that everyone you meet is fighting a battle you don't know anything about. So you put twenty-four hours into this?"

"Yeah."

"So what's forty take away twenty-nine?"

Matt stared, feeling panicked. "Um . . . what?"

"One hundred forty minus one hundred twenty-nine. Don't think of how big the numbers are. Just ignore the number one in front of the hundreds. Then count up from twenty-nine to forty. Twenty-nine, thirty, then ten more to make forty, right? That makes eleven the difference between them. Follow?"

"Yeah," Matt said, not positive he did. But ignoring the hundred did seem simpler.

When she passed Matt's page back, she was all business again. "Now hurry up! Get off my bus!" She winked.

What a strange lady, Matt thought.

He glanced down to see she had completed the math he'd started.

MATT'S SLED DOG SCHOOL BY MATT MISCO

Assets
dogsleds
harnesses
gang line
sled dogs

Expenses:
coveralls	$29
dog food ($20 x 5 dogs =)	$100
total:	$129

Sales (3 clients)
Tubbs	$50
Alex	$40 (4 weeks)
Flute	$50
total:	$140

	Debit	Credit
income		$140
expenses	$129	
total	$129	$140
net income:		$11

Total time to teach lessons
24 hours: 3 hours for every Saturday (5),
Sunday (1), Wednesday (1), and Friday (1)

Salary:
$11.00 net income ÷ 24 hours = $0.46 per hour

    Matt's salary made him cringe. He should've charged more. But then would he have gotten any clients?

    When he walked into math class, everyone came at him at once.

    "We saw your dogs on TV!" Tammy said. "They're so cute! I want to learn how. Can I take your lessons?"

    "I want to take lessons too," Destin said.

    "Me too. I want to sign up," Jen said, and she latched pinkies with Tammy as if they were doing it together.

    Matt blinked. Jacob stood behind everyone and glared

at Matt. "Watch out for Maniac Misco if you go over there," Jacob said.

But no one was paying attention to him. They all wanted to learn how to mush. The school project was over, but now Matt had his pick of clients. He couldn't stop the grin from spreading across his face.

"Everyone, settle down," Mr. Moffat said from his desk. "Come hand in your assignments and take a seat. We have guests today."

That shut everyone up. Chairs screeched on the floor as the students found their desks. Who were the guests?

Twenty-One

An excited whisper spread across the room as two guys walked in wearing leather and carrying laptops.

"Today we have Mark and Steven from MotorHeads."

A few cheers broke out around the room. Destin nudged Jacob teasingly.

"We started our business as a bike shop, repairing flat tires," Steven began. Matt listened to Steven explain how MotorHeads had grown. Steven went through their business plan, starting with who they were, what their product was, who their competition was, and their original marketing plan. They answered all the questions on Mr. Moffat's business plan list.

Matt glanced back at Mr. Moffat to see him busy marking papers. Matt gripped the side of his desk. What would Mr. Moffat say about his final assignment?

"Now comes the fun part: our finances." Mark started up this part of their presentation on the Smart Board screen like Tammy. The first PowerPoint slide showed the services they had started with:

SERVICES:
flat tire	$7.50
brakes	$25.00
tune-ups	$65.00

They showed graphs and explained their profit and loss statements. They talked about the local university contract for bike rentals, which helped them generate income, and their bike and clothing sales once they'd expanded.

When Matt saw the photos of their storefront, the bikes, the workshop, and then the expanded motorcycle section, he finally understood why all this mattered. Their workshop, with all the tools hanging neatly, reminded him of their barn at home. This was real life.

He recalled Tubbs pointing out how Matt was good

at cutting chicken into equal portions. How he could measure tug lines and calculate how much rope he'd need to cut. When it came to the dogs, Matt didn't mind doing the math.

With all the sudden interest in dogsledding, he wondered if he could make a successful business like MotorHeads. If he could do it as an actual job, like Mark and Steven did. But Matt would need to know how much to charge, to increase his salary. He'd have to make calculations for the profit and loss statements. Matt sat back in his chair as a thought hit him.

He actually *did* need help in this class.

He needed someone to explain things more clearly. Not like Mr. Moffat, who didn't have the time with all of the other students around. Not like Mrs. Wilson, who went too fast. But someone to show Matt how to use real-life math. And translate the totals to figure out the numbers on paper. Dividing a block of meat into twenty-two equal parts was easy. He just needed help with the book work.

How much more useful would the calculations be if he *did* go to the remedial class and then actually understood this stuff? Matt watched Mark and Steven hand out MotorHeads key chains and imagined how it would feel to be in math class without the dread.

At the end of class, Mr. Moffat told the students to come pick up their marked assignments. Matt was almost the last to his teacher's desk.

"Mr. Misco, why didn't you do this on a computer?"

"We don't have one at home, sir." Matt hardly ever used his lifestyle as an excuse and ducked his head to avoid meeting Mr. Moffat's eyes.

"Yes, well . . . that's what the computer lab is for. Next time ask me for help if you can't get to a school computer."

Matt opened his mouth to tell him that he did need help, but nothing came out. His heart pounded. His hands went clammy, and he suddenly felt as if he might throw up. Mr. Moffat handed him his assignment, and in a blink, Matt's chance was gone.

He glanced at the paper and read *"Good Effort"* in red ink in the top right corner. And then he saw the mark.

One hundred percent.

Twenty-Two

Matt didn't have much time.

"Haw," he called to Foo and Grover as they approached the fork in the trail. Their ears swiveled back but they didn't break stride. As usual, the dogs were being awesome.

Lily shrieked, as they skidded left around a poplar stand. At this speed they should make it to the mailbox in time to meet Mom. With five dogs in Matt's team now, the new rule, he felt as if they could run effortlessly right through to Canada.

Matt wanted to show her his project. No matter that he had had a little help from a crazy bus driver—he'd worked hard at his business. And now he wasn't going to fail math class.

They passed the tall pine. Rounding the bend, they could see the road and the row of mailboxes, and Mom getting out of her car.

"Yip-yip-yip!" Matt called to the team. They broke into a lope. The sled slid down the hill and they made it to the mailboxes just as Mom found her key.

"Jumping crickets, you startled me!" She beamed at them as the dogs dived into a snowbank for a break. "Whatcha seen, jellybeans?"

Matt had never been so anxious for her to ask that.

"The letter A." He smiled a bit smugly, adding, "For my math assignment."

"Wonderful." She wrapped Matt and Lily in a hug. "Let's see who can make it home first," she said.

And that was it. There was no difference in her reaction from when Matt normally got a C or worse. He tried not to let it bother him as he turned the dogs around to head back. But why wasn't she prouder?

✿ ✿ ✿

That night after story, Mom went into Matt's room. "Great job keeping your work ethic throughout your whole project. You put a lot of effort into sharing your talents."

"My talents?"

"Yes, your intuitive sense of how to do things. Don't you feel it? You tend to follow your instincts rather than rules. Not everyone has the ability to work out problems for themselves. And you started a business and handled the dogs, all while looking out for your sister."

He did work out problems. Just not math problems. Matt turned her words over in his mind as he plumped his pillow. "I guess I thought you'd be happier with my grade."

"Matthew, I'm happy no matter what marks you get in school. Grades put so much pressure on people. Education is about much more than going to school. It's about learning from your experiences."

Mom motioned for Matt to scootch over on the bed and sat next to him.

"I already know you're brilliant and capable and resourceful." She counted his attributes on her fingers. "But the best quality you have is how you promote what you love instead of following what most people do—complaining about what they hate. Those character traits are far more important than grades."

She ran her fingers through Matt's hair, brushing it off his forehead. "Life skills will help you succeed in everything you set your mind to."

"Mom, what do you think about the remedial math class? I don't really understand the numbers. I think . . . The teacher didn't tell me I have to go or anything. I'm just wondering if I should."

"Oh," she said in a voice so tiny, he barely heard her.

She gathered him into a hug. But it felt like a different kind of hug. She held him and held him until all the worry he'd carried about his marks got squeezed out. It came out his eyes, and before he knew it, his face was wet. He felt so much better.

"I'm so very proud you've asked me that. It takes bravery to ask for help and admit when we don't know something." She pulled back and beamed. "I'll make some calls and get it set up."

Twenty-Three

"Flute's been wondering when he can go running again," Tubbs said on the phone the next day. "I think he misses Atlas."

"Yeah, I think Atlas misses him, too."

"So, should we come over? I know the sled school is done, but . . . I'm wondering . . . if we can maybe hang out this Saturday."

"I was going to suggest it. I have something to talk to you about."

As soon as Matt hung up, he phoned Alex. He hoped this idea worked.

Saturday morning, Alex and Tubbs arrived in the yard as planned. The dogs knew their cars, so they didn't even bother barking. But they ran around in circles, eager to get on the trail.

"Meeting in the barn first," Matt said.

Alex and Tubbs shrugged and followed Matt.

"Here's the thing," Matt said, once they'd settled in the barn. "I've got tons of new clients who want to sign up for sledding lessons. But I can't do it alone. I'm looking for some business partners."

If MotorHeads started with just two guys and a bike shop, Matt had a good feeling about three friends and a dog team.

Tubbs and Alex glanced at each other.

"These partners," Matt continued, "would both need to be junior musher graduates. And be obsessive about outhouses. And sometimes need to quote Latin subspecies. Do you know anyone like that?"

Tubbs waved his hand. "Hey! I like outhouses! *And* I'm a junior musher!"

Alex met Matt's eyes and held out her hand. "What's the pay like?"

Matt shook her hand. "Terrible."

"I'm in."

"Me too!" Tubbs said, hopping up from his seat to do a little jig.

Matt shook his hand too.

"I can do the book work," Tubbs said. "I'm good in math."

Matt gripped Tubbs's hand and stared at him.

"What? If that's a bad idea, I don't have to. I just like doing problems. I know you're good in math too. Can I . . . can I have my hand back?"

"You like *problems?*" Matt couldn't believe it. He could've asked Tubbs for help this whole time.

"I just play around with them on my computer. I love numbers. But if you don't want me to, that's okay. I'm just happy to be a partner! Our own business! A dogsledding business!" He hopped at the end of every sentence.

"How about you teach me how to solve math problems and we can do the book work together?" Matt said.

"Deal!"

Lily burst through the barn door, trailed by the pups tussling with Bandit. "Did I miss anything? What are you talking about? Can I come?"

Matt grinned at his sister and felt as if he finally understood the "Advice from a Sled Dog" poster. This was his pack. It felt good to work as a team. "Who wants to go for a run?" he said.

Glossary of Terms

Alaskan husky—A mixed breed of dog with bloodlines originating in Alaska and bred for speed, toughness, and endurance.

Basket sled—A type of wooden dogsled with an elevated basket on stanchions. Short basket sleds are generally used for racing.

Chase team—A sled dog team following closely behind the leading team.

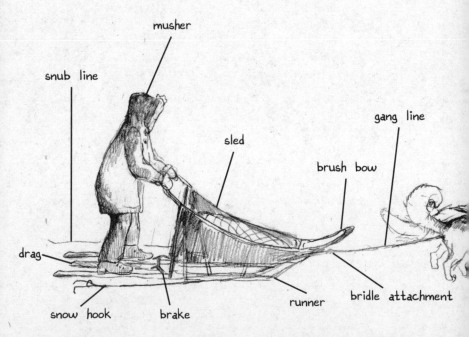

Dog yard—The area where the dogs are kept either in kennels or staked out with chains that allow each dog to run in a circle around the stake.

Drag—A piece of snowmobile track or tire that rests between the runners. A musher steps on it to slow down the team.

Gang line—The line that attaches to the dogsled with a bridle and runs between the dogs. All the sled dogs are attached to the gang line in pairs or singly.

"Gee"—A command to turn right.

Half-hitch knot—A quick-release knot used by some mushers to secure the snub line so that it is easily released under pressure by pulling on one end.

wheel dogs

point or swing dogs

tug line

lead dogs

Handlebar—The curved or square bar at the back of the sled that a musher holds on to.

"Haw"—A command to turn left.

"Hike up"—A command sometimes used to ask the sled dogs to begin running. Some mushers will just say, "Ready? All right!"

Leaders—The sled dogs at the front of the gang line who listen to the musher and guide the team.

Musher—A person who runs sled dogs.

Neckline—A line attached to the gang line that clips onto a dog's collar to keep the dog facing forward.

Point—The position in the gang line directly behind the leaders. Also called **swing**.

Sled bag—A fitted bag made with heavy coated nylon material that is tied to the inside of a sled basket.

Sled basket—The area inside either a basket sled or a toboggan sled that holds the load.

Snow hook—A heavy metal claw attached by a rope to the gang line, designed to dig into the snow when the team pulls to keep them temporarily in place.

Snub line—A rope attached to the bridle that runs along the dogsled and is tied to an unmovable object such as a tree to anchor the team.

Stanchion—A vertical supporting piece of wood in the frame of a dogsled.

Swing—The position in the gang line directly behind the lead dogs. Also called **point**.

Toboggan sled—A type of dogsled with a flat-bottomed base usually made from heavy plastic that is designed to carry loads (such as passengers and/or gear) and slide over the top of the snow.

"Trail"—A command from one musher to another, to signal that the team behind is about to pass and to ask the lead team to move over on the trail.

Tug line—Connects the back of a dog's harness to the gang line. This is how the dog's power is transferred to the sled.

Wheel—The position in the gang line directly in front of the dogsled. Wheel dogs take the brunt of the load in the sled. They also steer the sled by pulling it around corners.

"Whoa"—A command to slow down or stop.

"Yip-yip-yip"—A command to ask the dogs to go faster.

Acknowledgments

Sled Dog School began as a ten-page-per-week writing pact with Kiki Hamilton, who is most likely the reason that this story became a book. Thank you, Kiki, for being the first to believe!

Thank you to my critique partners and early readers: Amy Fellner Dominy, Marcia Wells, Sylvia Musgrove, Jenn Marie Thorne, and Jackie White.

Thank you to my incredible partner, Denis, who does everything else *but* read, including showing me how to whittle, explaining the mindset of boys, and providing a patient ear and sounding board for endless hours of brainstorming.

And a special thank-you to a few brave teachers, who took time out from their summer vacations to help me with my math: Patty Lea, Kelly and Peter Ahlfeld, and Davette Nixon. Also thanks to Karen Upper for her help. Any errors in this novel are mine.

And finally, I am forever grateful for the love, dedication, and trust of my sled dogs. They taught me many life lessons while we shared adventures on the trails together: Apollo, Elsie, Soho, Denali, Tarzan, Mukluk, Sitka, Ulu, Destiny, Blaze, Jade, Orbit, Doppler, Nitro, Gonzo, Vinny, Little Doe, and Belle. Also Tundra, Taiga, and Tanzer. Good dogs. I miss you all.

Yes, Denali, that part about the soul connection, that was about you.

About the Author

Terry Lynn Johnson works as a conservation officer in northern Ontario. Before that she was a wilderness park ranger, canoeing in Quetico Provincial Park during the summer months and running her eighteen sled dogs during the winter.

Terry began her mushing journey as a dog handler. She worked for several different mushers assisting at races, and taking out clients on dogsled expeditions. For the first years she focused on learning everything she could about how to care for and train the dogs. Her apprenticeship began in Thunder Bay, Ontario, and took her to Minnesota and Alaska.

When she was ready for her own dogs, she started with a small kennel of five Alaskan huskies. She raced in a few events and usually came in last or second to last. But racing was fun because it was where she could meet with other mushers. It was the best place to be able to talk endlessly about everything dog. "Who are you running this year in lead?" "How are those yearlings doing?" "Have you tried this foot ointment?" "How much are you feeding?" "When are you feeding?" "What are you feeding?"

Terry never tired of dogs, the same as any musher who has owned a team. They are the center of any musher's life. Every single dog needs attention and time. Owning a team means that most of a musher's resources and energy goes toward keeping them happy and healthy. When Terry wasn't running dogs, she was dreaming about them, or talking about them.

A few years later, Terry figured out the real joy of running dogs was just being on the trail with them. Her kennel grew. Soon she had acquired a few more adults and also bred a litter of pups, which would become the core of her team. She began to give dogsled rides, and enjoyed sharing the experience with others. She taught dogsledding at the Kingfisher Outdoor School in Thunder Bay to fifth- and sixth-graders. She also ran dogs with Outward Bound in northern Ontario.

Once she became a conservation officer, Terry didn't have the time to properly care for her team, so she gave them up to another recreational musher who loved them as much as she did. Now Terry writes about dogsledding instead.

The lasting impact of working with those eighteen huskies wasn't how Terry trained the dogs to run as a team, but what they taught her—about pushing yourself, being enthusiastic, living life fully and in the moment. Most of all, they taught her about joy.

Visit Terry at www.terrylynnjohnson.com to see photos of some of her dogs.

FOR MORE MUSHING ADVENTURES, be sure to check out **Terry Lynn Johnson's** gripping survival tale *Ice Dogs*:

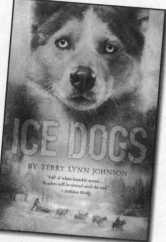

- 2015 Children's Choice Book Award Finalist
- 2014 Cybils Award Finalist
- A Junior Library Guild Selection
- American Booksellers Association Best Children's Books of 2014

"A page-turner full of white-knuckle action. . . . Readers will be riveted until the end." —*Publishers Weekly*

"[A] thoroughly engaging and incredibly suspenseful survival story. . . . Well-crafted, moving, and gripping." —*Kirkus Reviews*

"Debut novelist Johnson links character to setting by showing how Vicky uses her knowledge of the land and copes with the elements, creates shelter, and snares animals in order to survive." —*Horn Book*

"The high-stakes adventure and episodic nature of the chapters will make this book an easy sell for reluctant readers." —*School Library Journal*

Turn the page

for a sneak peek of

DOG DRIVEN

CHAPTER 1

Whoever's behind me is coming fast.

I peek over my shoulder and see a blurry line of shapes bearing down. Mustard glances back too, then faces forward and digs in. He's so cocky. He hates getting passed.

An unspoken message travels through the whole team and they surge forward together. I love how the speed comes up through my feet. Cold air darts through cracks in my neck warmer. I squint into the wind.

"Gee over, Mustard. Don't be rude. Attagirl, Twix."

I have an eight-dog team, so my front-runners are at the edge of my visual range. All I can see of my leaders are furry shapes. It's as though my sunglasses are coated in Vaseline. The bright sun compounds the issue. When it reflects off the snow, it hurts my eyes, even with my dark shades.

The sound of synchronized panting grows louder behind me.

"Trail!" a boy's voice calls.

I have just enough time to angle my sled to the right before his dogs come loping up beside me. They move along my sled, then shoulder past it to my dogs.

Saga and Haze both stick their faces directly in the way, stretching their necks for a good sniff. I cringe. Sixteen dogs running this close beside one another at ten miles an hour can make a nice tangled ball in a blink.

"Ahead!" I call, trying to keep the embarrassment out of my voice. Why can't my dogs behave like everyone else's when we're out in public? I'm driving savages. I watch the other team. Focused ahead, no nonsense, passing like pros.

I stare at the musher as he glides by. He's near my age, or maybe a little older. And he's wearing some kind of war uniform that looks like it came out of his great-grandfather's closet.

"Ma'am," he says. He doesn't even watch his dogs to make sure they're going straight, just turns backwards on the runners and bows at me. *Bows.*

"Hey, Retro," I call. "Why bother? Now I'm going to have to pass you!"

He laughs and then he's out of my range. I'm left with the sounds of the trail—the *shush* of the runners gliding over sun-softened snow, then the clacking noise they make on the harder, shaded sections of trail. The necklines tinkle, and the wind whistles. I could never run this fast on my own. Never feel the clean bite of air filling up my nostrils. Filling *me* up.

I'm never as free as I am out here behind this team.

My gaze roves up and down my dogs. Sumo's dipping snow already but keeping pace. The fluorescent strips I've stitched along the backs of the dog harnesses make them stand out, especially on white dogs like Damage and Haze. Without the strips I can hardly tell them from a snowbank. But the real trouble will start at dusk, when everything turns into black blobs, fluorescent strips or not.

A wide-open expanse appears. My team goes down the bank and then moves onto the frozen lake. There's a commotion ahead; I hear it before I see it. Two mushers are yelling.

"Grab your leaders!"

"Sorry! I'm sorry!"

Dogs barking.

Their teams flounder in the snow. I arrive just as the dogfight breaks out. I throw down my snow hook, wondering what to do next. Should I go help? No, I'll surely give myself away, stumbling over dogs.

My team shrieks and lunges to get closer to the action. I'm hesitant to leave the sled in case Sumo pops the hook and we have three teams tangled. But I can't tell what's going on from back here. I creep closer, moving up beside my leaders. The mushers are grabbing armfuls of dogs and tugs.

"They wouldn't listen!" A girl wearing yellow wind pants struggles with a dog as if she's never untangled a dog team before.

"What are you doing?" It's the retro boy who passed me. "Unclip the tug or my dog will get pinched!"

"This one?"

"No, your point dog! Hurry! Yoda, enough!"

His wheel dog, not even in the tangle, is screaming so loud now, it's hard for me to think. Which is why I dive into the fray.

I reach for the girl's leggy point dog, flicking off my mitts as I do so my bare fingers are ready. Once I've grabbed the dog, I go by instinct. Unclip the tug, flip the line under, then reclip her dog. It's all automatic and takes about two seconds.

The line is still tangled.

I walk backwards a few steps with the tugs, straightening the leaders, and squint at the gangline. There. A neckline needs to be unclipped. Once I've got the leaders untangled, I have to hold the leggy dog's collar to prevent him from turning around. It's satisfying to know that my dogs aren't the worst brats ever.

I peer at my team but can see only a line of crazed, hopping mongrels. I'm too far away to tell if the snow hook is coming loose. *Please don't come loose.*

My feet sink through the crust of snow and I slop around in slush. "You want to get them going," I tell the girl. "I'll hold them out."

She seems to suddenly come out of her fog and leaps onto her sled.

"Hike up!" she yells, and the dogs pitch forward, picking up speed. Her sled zips past me, throwing up a rooster tail of slush.

"Thanks," the boy says. "I think she's new."

I feel a nose shoving at my butt. I turn and recognize the black and silver markings of the boy's lead dog. But then I do a double take and peer closer. Her eyes! "What's wrong with your dog?"

"What?" The boy looks up, then relaxes. "Oh, you mean Zesty. Yeah, she's blind as a bat. Anyway, thanks for your help."

"You . . . your lead dog . . . you have a *blind* lead dog?"

"She's the best. Hey, love to chat, but should we get going? You know. *Race.*"

I peer intently into Zesty's face. She's focused on the departing team, ears erect, body tightly coiled. She appears to be watching, but her eyes are fully clouded over. She swivels her face toward me as if sensing I'm staring.

"Your team!"

I jerk my gaze up. The boy lunges for my sled as it shoots past him. His feet get bogged down in the slush. He misses.

I have one chance. I try to line myself in the right place but it's going to be tight. I can't see the sled clearly, and my depth perception is off. How close is it? Where is that handlebar? My dogs rush past me as I lean over, desperate, reaching . . . reaching.

Bam!

My bent arm hooks the handlebar. I swing up onto the runners. Step on the brake. Lean down to where the snow hook should be. There it is. Snag it up. Set it in its cradle. Straighten, focus ahead. Adrenaline still pumping.

I can feel my dogs smiling from here.

I told him I'd pass him.

December 7, 1896

Dear Margaret,

I leave the port of Killarney on the morrow with the mail courier Raymond Miron and his team of dogs. There is wild beauty here with windswept pines and stark white cliffs, but also loneliness. I miss home terribly. Alas, the Hudson's Bay Company requires me at White River upon the most haste, and I shall endeavor to comply . . . Love to little Anna. She will be grown enough to beat me in a horserace when I return.

Your loving brother, William

CHAPTER 2

Two months before the race

I open the puppy pen's metal door with a creak, and our three yearlings from last year's litter explode past me.

Their frenetic energy rarely fails to cheer me up, but this time I stand next to the pen, a shovel in hand, and peer at the door in dismay.

When we first built the pen, Mom painted BARNEY KEN-NELS in bright red across the door. Though it's faded now, the letters are still stark against the pattern of dog-paw prints she'd added in blue. It's the same pattern as the trim in my little sister's old bedroom. I've always been jealous of it. The trouble is, I can no longer see the pattern.

For the past few months I've let myself believe that perhaps I just need glasses. Glasses or something else, maybe corrective surgery, and I'll be all fixed. However, living with Emma, I know the signs.

Last month, I could still see the pattern. Today, it has slipped behind a spot in the center of my vision. I close one eye. The little off-center patch in my vision has grown over the past few weeks. It's slightly purple and distorted, like when you press on your eyeball and see sparkles. When I open that eye and close the other one, the spot moves. I open both eyes, and the spot now meets in the center of my vision. I've been tracking where the distorted spot appears. Up to now, when both eyes were open, I could still see in the center. It's happened so fast. And because of how fast it happened, I know.

I clutch the smooth wooden handle of the shovel. There is no denying it any longer. I have it. A hot bubble of fear and grief swells inside me. *How can I live with this?*

I hear Mom and Emma pulling into the driveway. "I'm in the yard," I call out, eager for a distraction.

"McKenna! Oh my God!" Em's voice, quivering with excitement. "You'll never guess!"

"The yearlings are loose!" I warn Mom as the pups thunder past me.

Emma comes into view, holding on to the crook of Mom's

arm as they make their way to me. She's not even bothering with her cane. Again.

The yearlings turn and gallop back, biting each other's necks, not looking where they're going. But they somehow avoid plowing into my sister and continue on a loop around the fence line.

I wait till Emma comes close. "Good day at school?" I ask.

"There's gonna be a new dogsled race in Sault Ste. Marie, Ontario. It's called the Great Superior Mail Run," Emma says, speaking quickly as she releases her grip on Mom. "Mushers carry real mail in their sleds so it gets stamped with *Delivered by Dog Team* on it! And guess what — our class is going to write letters! They can be to anyone."

"That sounds cool," I say.

The yearlings arrive at my feet in a pile, growling and mock fighting. They have the whole dog yard to run around in, but apparently they need an audience. Their faces are covered in one another's goober, which is beginning to freeze stiff like hair gel. Suddenly they leap up and go tearing off again full throttle.

Emma giggles as she turns her head to the side to see them. "I bet if I wrote the Foundation for Fighting Blindness and asked them for more research on Stargardt disease, they'd *have* to do it. It would stand out from all the other mail with the stamp on it. I mean, duh, right? And then I bet it'll be on TV. Everyone would hear about Stargardt's and want to donate money for research."

It's my sister's simple view of the world. The research for a cure needs to be done, so everyone should care about it.

"Right." I glance at Mom uneasily. I hope this isn't going where I think it's going.

"And they'd for sure put it on TV when they find out it's my *sister* who's delivering it!" Em waves her arms around like a dork, flapping her fleece gloves, and I have to smile despite the dread that's lodged in my gut.

I look to Mom again, grasping for a lifeline, but she has no idea what's going on with me. She nods as if to say of course I'm racing it. I realize they've already talked about this and now I'm ambushed.

"The dogs would love a stage race like this," Mom says. "You've run them so much this season, they're in top form. And it's a great idea to help your sister. We could all use a bit of hope, don't you think, McKenna?"

Mom takes my shovel. She's trying to bridge the gap of silence that's grown between us lately, but I don't know how to cross it. There's an awkward little moment when our eyes meet, but then I look away. She sighs and starts cleaning the yard where I left off.

"But they wouldn't let the junior mushers carry the mail," I say — and then almost get knocked off my feet from behind when two of the three nerds barrel into the backs of my legs. "Watch it!"

"That's the perfect part," Emma says. "This race is open to mushers fourteen and up, so you'll just make it! Juniors race with adults!"

Em carefully takes the two steps to Sumo's doghouse and leans her butt against it. She claps softly, and the big dog rests his chin on her thigh. I have no idea how he knows not to jump up on her, but it's probably the reason she adores him. He's a gentle giant. Until he's running in the team — then he's a steam engine.

Emma continues. "The race is like a celebration of dogsledding because they used to bring stuff to the towns by dog team. It's important to history. That's why my teacher wants us to be part of it. She said the Canadian dogsled mail run was like the Pony Express here in the States. Can you believe it? Everyone in my class was talking about how amazing dogsledding is!"

And there's the reason she wants me to run it. Because she can't. Suddenly, all her friends are interested in dogsledding, and wouldn't it be great if she were the star of her class for once? My heart cracks.

You'd think for someone who gets everything done for her, she'd be bratty. But that's the thing about Em. She's so sweet that it makes you want to do things for her all the time. She's not like most kids her age. Maybe because she's been through so much crap already. Hardship makes you tough. She doesn't take kindness for granted or expect stuff from people, like big gifts or trips to Disney.

Since she was young when the symptoms began, only six, it took a while to get the diagnosis from the retina specialist. I can never forget that visit when we were told what it was. Having so many different tests in one day traumatized my whole family. And in the two years since then, her disease has quickly worsened.

She has some sight. Most people don't know there are levels of sight impairment. Her last exam showed she's 20/600, worse than last year, when she was 20/200, which is legally blind. I hate that it's labeled like that because it's so confusing. She's not *blind* just because she can't see that stupid letter at the top of the eye chart anymore. She can see better in her peripheral vision.

Before I started worrying about crashing, I used to take her out with me in my sled all the time because she made it so fun. Her excitement over the wind in her face, the motion of going fast. She would love to be able to mush a team on her own. But she can't run like she used to. She only has me to run her dogs for her.